DEVON C. FORD
ADVERSITY

AETHON BOOKS

ADVERSITY

©2019 DEVON C. FORD

Dedicated to Baby J, who at the time of first writing this was no longer trying to recreate the chest-bursting scene from Alien, but instead wanted to chat loudly throughout the night...

ALSO IN THE SERIES

Toy Soldiers:

Apocalypse

Aftermath

Abandoned

You're reading: Adversity

Books five and six yet to be named (coming 2019)

PREFACE

All spelling and grammar in this book is UK English except for proper nouns and those American terms which just don't anglicize.

PROLOGUE

FEBRUARY 1990

The two of them, a man and one woman, drove almost silently down the sloping entranceway, the engine cut and the driver fighting the wheel as he feathered the brakes. They weren't so ill-trained, so lacking in awareness, as to drive straight up to the front entrance and wander around aimlessly, so they had parked nearby and crept in on foot to observe the big structure and its large enclosed yard, having recently been uncomfortably forced into awareness of enemies both living and dead.

They had watched for an hour, all of them accustomed to long periods of stillness, with total concentration and discipline, until they were satisfied that nobody was holding or defending the area. In broad daylight, the assumption that at least some movement would be evident reassured them that it was indeed empty. No sentries showed themselves to piss against a wall or smoke as they stretched their legs. No sounds came from the area at all. One of them wore a beard, shorter than it had been before, but he'd felt compelled to trim it down as the ragged length it had grown to had begun to interfere with his tactical abilities. This man rose slowly to his feet and stayed low. The slimmer figure twenty paces to his right rose at the same time, her smaller frame bulked out with layered clothing in contrast to the bearded man's mass being mostly meat. He had lost some of his bulk over the months prior, mostly due to the reason they were there in the first place; namely a lack of food. The inability to train with heavy weights four or five times each week, and the struggle to maintain his usual high-calorie intake had taken the edge off his intimidating physique, but not to the point where he was small or weak, by any stretch of the imagination.

The woman was wearing the layers of clothing against the cold, a black woollen scarf wrapped tightly around the lower part of her face, allowing only the slightest puff of warm breath to escape when she spoke in a low voice.

"Overwatch?" she asked simply in slightly accented English, making her suggestion sound like a question, understanding well enough at the same time how her partner thought, to know that he had no qualms about sharing the responsibility of command. At their level of operating, or at least who and what they used to be back in the world, command was a fluid concept, as whoever made it to their team would be capable of leading, regardless of rank.

The eyes above the beard and below the woolly hat pulled down over his brow met hers briefly, before he turned and pointed two fingers at his face with an exaggerated movement. No response came, but he knew that the immobile sniper would have seen his gesture from the tangled branches of the tree he was occupying.

Satisfied that the heavy-calibre rifle covered their approach, the two moved forward, weapons up and tucked into shoulders, as one advanced while the other took a knee to cover their approach in small leapfrog moves. Black boots crunched on fresh frost which still hadn't thawed, despite the sun having risen in the sky above the low cloud cover. They opened the front doors of the car they had been using since the van from their small village stronghold had given up the ghost mid-mission, both putting their shoulders to the doorframes as the man reached in to put the key in the ignition to free the steering lock and release the handbrake. As soon as they had built a little momentum, they both timed their steps to jump inside and fold their bodies into the seats and pull the doors in with a soft click, as they were instinctively mindful enough not to slam them shut.

The noise of the tyres rolling on the pitted concrete sounded unnaturally loud in the environment they had spent a silent hour in, followed by a shriek of rusted brake pads on drums as he pressed harder on the brake pedal to slow their approach.

———

From his position in the old oak tree almost two hundred paces away, the man lying between the branches like a big cat with his right eye pressed to the scope of the Accuracy International rifle winced at the noise. A high-pitched squeal like that could be heard for half a mile in all directions, but hopefully the heavy tree cover in the area would cancel out how far the sound had travelled in the thin, cold air. Snow began to fall, only lightly, but enough to obscure the tracks the others had made.

He hadn't changed position in over twenty minutes, and even then, the shift was subtle and very slowly done. He was a professional, a term that many people used, but when it was applied to the skill set of a person trained and experienced in killing people at a distance when given a shot window of seconds in a mission lasting hours or days, the word barely seemed adequate. It wasn't just his uncanny ability to know how to naturally and instinctively correct his aim for the path of the bullet being affected by so many factors, but it was more that his personality suited his chosen skill set perfectly; he was unnervingly calm and noiseless and moved like a ghost. His natural quietness had deepened over the last months, ever since the death of his closest friend and spotter. The two had joined the Royal Marines together and both attended and passed the same sniper training course, and one without the other was only part of a whole. That wasn't to say that the immobile man in the tree wasn't a devastating instrument of warfare in his own right, but he was only part of the equation and would probably never feel entire again.

All of these background thoughts only took up a tiny portion of his consciousness, as his focus was on both his two friends rolling the ugly, off-brown Austin Montego down the ramp towards the big building inside the fenced enclosure. Even though his eye was pressed to the scope, his other eye remained open and fed a second visual input into his brain, such was his natural ability to multitask. He watched the two of them stack up as a pair, drilling their CQB – close-quarter battle – methods flawlessly, despite only having the number of half a patrol that the tactics were designed for. He watched as the man reached for the familiar shape of the crowbar tucked down the back of the thick jacket that his webbing was worn over. The slightest splintering crack of wood reached the sniper's ears over the distance, just after he saw the corresponding body movements used to wrench open the door.

Seeing them both disappear inside, flicking on the large Maglite torches attached to the fat barrels of their compact weapons, he watched as Astrid and Bufford disappeared inside.

And he waited.

———

"Ready?" Buffs asked softly of Astrid, who had pulled down the scarf so that her mouth was exposed to the cold air. Her breath misted as Bufford's did, only hers wasn't filtered by the scruffy facial hair.

"Go," she said faintly, following his lead as the two of them poured into the building like water. They split left and right, powerful torch beams flashing around the darkened interior to create crazy shadows between the tall aisles. The beams of light, pointing in every direction that their weapon barrels and eyes did, showed how alert they were to the possibility of unwanted company as they moved anti-clockwise around the inner perimeter of the warehouse, until they eventually returned to the door where they had made their entry. At the centre of the warehouse was a single construction surrounded by an open area before the tall ranks of industrial shelves. That area contained three small forklift trucks and appeared to be the office which ran the distribution for the area. Each of the long, wide aisles contained wrapped pallets of foodstuffs; bags of dried pasta and rice, as well as large tins of beans and tomatoes. The company logo outside the large roller shutter doors meant nothing to them, but the contents made it obvious that the warehouse provided for the catering and commercial markets.

Bufford dropped to one knee as Astrid automatically turned to adopt the same pose facing away from him.

"See if the truck works?" he asked her softly, "Load it and take it back?"

"This is a good idea," she replied, her grasp of English being almost flawless but lending her a formal tone. She gave the accurate impression of being classroom taught, as opposed to the colloquial use of the language by a native speaker, but that wasn't to say that she wasn't picking up a few choice terms that her training didn't cater for. Her Russian was less formal, but her Cold War training hadn't required her to blend in with the population on the UK mainland.

Bufford went to rise but froze as a noise behind him sounded muffled in the dusty gloom.

"Office," Astrid said.

Bufford gave no verbal answer, rising instead and turning to follow her lead as she approached the door. He flicked his thumb all the way up on the fire selector, pushing it from single shot to safe, and let the gun hang down as he reached behind his right hip to draw the peculiar weapon he carried. He had never been awarded or issued the assault pioneer's axe, a throwback of British military tradition, and especially odd to his hands as it was an idiosyncrasy of the army and not from his naval roots. But he had taken it on a whim from the sergeants' mess display on the base he had found himself occupying when the world had so suddenly turned to shit. He didn't know why he had taken it, but he was glad a dozen times over that he had. He drew it now, its polished head glinting off the weapon-mounted light of Astrid's MP5 as she stood by the door and looked at him, waiting for his nod.

He gave it, crouching low beside the doorway as she spun the handle and stepped smartly backwards to give a distance of nearly fifteen feet, where she froze with her gun raised and ready. Nothing happened immediately, but the groaning and banging from inside in response to their presence told them that one of them was in there. Slowly reanimating, having likely been immobile in the strange hibernating state they adopted when cold and undisturbed, the Screecher inside shambled towards the light and noise. And seeing the weapon-mounted light, it broke into a run.

Astrid, with a clear line of sight, fought against the very natural urge to drill a 9mm round straight through the grey-skinned skull of the beast that opened its mouth and reached for her, taking fast but unsteady steps towards her on legs that had stayed still for too long. Her torch beam illuminated the face, cloudy eyes not responding to the harsh light as a living person would. She kept her discipline, not wanting to waste a single, precious bullet, as they were running out at a rate that was unsustainable, and she held her breath as it reached the threshold and took a longer step out of the room.

As it did, Bufford rose to bring the axe down one-handed in a savage blow that crushed the skull and crumpled the former worker to the concrete floor like a meat concertina. Using his foot to hold the ruined head still, he pulled the axe away and wiped it on the torso just as a single word cut across his concentration.

"Buffs!" Astrid snapped desperately.

He didn't think, simply abandoned the position to throw himself out of arms reach and roll back to his feet as two snapping coughs tore the air. He looked back to see another one, female, tall and heavily built, fall like a tree as the second bullet snapped her head back. He watched as though in slow-motion, the adrenaline in his body slowing the real-time events of the world briefly, as her body moved like the footage of crash test dummies on television. Her head flew back, whipping forwards with the momentum of her skull and upper spine going through their full range of movement, to go rigid and topple forwards to land with a meaty thud on top of the one he had dispatched, or had *rendered safe*, as one of their companions said, and she lay motionless.

Bufford looked at Astrid and nodded once, the sincere thanks and the returning acknowledgement passing between them in an effortless flash of non-verbal communication. He rose, dusted himself off and slipped the axe back into his belt before they cleared the small office. The stench they had remembered from the early days was gone, replaced by an almost sickly sweetness of dried-out meat that had gone off.

The cold had changed everything as soon as the unexpectedly freezing winter had set in for real, and despite battling the constant chill and hunger, at least the zombies were easier to deal with. The office held little of worth apart from the warm coats which were superfluous to their needs, but the keys to the single box truck preserved inside the warehouse made them both breathe a sigh of relief that they wouldn't have to search the pockets of the twice-dead corpses.

Rolling up the rear doors, they found the truck half-stocked with sacks containing either rice or flour – they couldn't be sure which, and neither did they overly care – so they returned to the aisles to use their knives to remove the heavy plastic wrapping from pallets and retrieve heavy can after heavy can of beans and soup. They loaded as much as they dared, both having to strip off their thick coats as they rapidly overheated with the exercise, and seemed to simultaneously feel that they had pushed their luck enough with the time they had been there. They knew that their guard outside would never complain, but he would only remain on-station for so long before he climbed down from his perch with the big rifle slung across his back and follow them inside; such was their curse with a lack of personal communications.

Using the keys to check that the battery still held charge, Astrid flicked the ignition on and off once to give Bufford a thumbs-up gesture from inside the cab. They moved back to the door where they had entered, stepping out cautiously as they knew the long barrel of a high-powered rifle would be aimed in their direction, and Bufford stood tall to make the signal for 'form on me' as he placed his left hand on his head with his fingers pointed down like some comedy interpretation of a spider coming to rest on his dome. He held the pose for ten seconds to make sure that he had been seen, then crouched to adopt a defensive position.

Inside a minute Enfield joined them, his newly-acquired small calibre rifle in hand and the longer barrel of his Accuracy International protruding over his right shoulder. He jogged towards them silently, slipping across the open space like the ghost he was, and fell in beside the SBS man.

"Truck loaded with catering supplies," Bufford said softly with undisguised happiness, "way too much for one haul. Lock this place up and come back with more hands," he finished. Enfield gave no reply, simply held his hands out for the keys to the car they had found on their way to the warehouse, which Bufford handed over.

"Roller shutter on that side," he told the marine as he pointed off to their right, "we'll go in front and you follow."

The same two slipped back inside and Enfield waited, hearing the laboured sounds of a neglected engine clatter and groan into life before he safetied his weapon and ran low for the door of the Montego. Suppressing a shudder as he slipped behind the wheel, he pushed the seat forward and turned the key with his foot on the clutch to reduce the stress of starting the tired engine. Vehicle travel was something they tried to avoid, but the unexpectedly harsh winter was pushing them to more desperate measures in their need to stay fed. He wound down the driver's window despite the cold, so that he could hear some of what was going on outside. He could hear the metal roller shutter protesting at being forced to open, like a teenager being made to get out of bed at sunrise, and he slipped the car into gear to fall in behind them at a distance where he would not become tangled up in any drama which might befall them.

They had food, finally, and they were heading back to their little slice of fortified Britain. Being abandoned by the rest of the world, however much of it still remained as before, times were becoming very hard.

ONE

FOUR MONTHS PRIOR

Captain Palmer sat at the desk in the ground floor room of their adopted and adapted country manor and rubbed his tired face with his hands. His stubbled cheeks rasped against his skin, as like almost all of the men, he had forgone the routine of shaving out of a simple lack of water and toiletries. The former Captain of the Household Cavalry, more accustomed to the challenges of armoured warfare than he was the vagaries of logistical concerns, wished that there was someone else to take on the task that had fallen to him.

The few of them who still shaved, despite the outrage of the Colonel, favoured the traditional method of using a straight-bladed razor instead of the more common disposable kind. With close to a hundred people in their group, a steady supply of such luxury items was so far down the list of priorities that they weren't worth expending any effort over.

His exasperation came from simple mathematics, as he calculated the number of mouths to feed versus the stores of food they had. Their scavenging missions usually followed the template of their SAS team scouting the area, and their remaining Royal Marines and men of the armoured Yeomanry squadron going in en-masse to clear out whatever was available. He knew that there was a booming trade in the black market going on at the house, and even he had lowered himself, via a trusted corporal, and traded a few items for things that he wanted. But his men knew better than to withhold food from the haul. Or at least he hoped for their sake that they did.

Their strange amalgamation of mixed armed services personnel and civilians rescued from the area had evolved over the few months that they had been there, but as a mild autumn began to give way to a sudden and brutally unkind winter, things had become increasingly difficult. He sat in the room, glancing forlornly at the empty fireplace and wishing that there were sufficient fuel stores to have even a small blaze to heat the room. He sighed loudly, uncharacteristically betraying his feelings, and tucked his chin deeper into the large uniform smock he still insisted on wearing, despite the multiple layers he wore underneath, including a thick, knitted jumper to insulate against the chill.

People often spoke of the onset of winter being sudden, but this year had been the worst in his memory and the cold was worse than the many skiing excursions his family had taken him on as a child. Pipes froze solid overnight, cracking the old brass open like a hatching egg and sparking terror as people ran around the large house looking for anyone with plumbing experience. By the time such a man had been located and roused from his bed, the flooding had caused extensive damage to the old carpets and the floorboards beneath. The floor below cascaded water through the cracked plaster ceiling to elicit shrieks of fear and discomfort from those suffering from the unnatural indoor rain, and what came after was worse still.

Because of the pandemonium and ensuing need for lights to be switched on during darkness, an operational cardinal sin, the house attracted unwelcome attention from the outside which raged on throughout the freezing night and into the morning. That single, costly night had taken a significant toll on their lives in the form of half of their remaining ammunition being expended and claiming the lives of three defenders. They still hadn't recovered from those losses, and morale at the house had plummeted into a deep depression.

Thinking again of the long and confusing engagement, Palmer tried to find the positives as well as ruthlessly assessing their defensive performance and plans. The wide ditch they had dug surrounding the vulnerable approaches to the house had undoubtedly saved them from being overrun, as had the bitterly cold weather which the area was unused to experiencing. They had found that from autumn, the number of Screechers wandering around had reduced exponentially, and those who did wander up to their defensive lines in ones and twos were rotting and sluggish, far worse than they had seen them deteriorate through summer.

On that night, when fate conspired with bad luck to deal them a cruel blow, they came in waves until entire sections of the ditches filled with bodies and allowed the shambling attackers to step over the writhing, struggling bodies to walk almost unimpeded towards the warm flesh of the men and women under Palmer's charge. Palmer was an officer of Her Majesty's Armed Forces, an officer trained at Sandhurst, which in his opinion, provided the finest officer training in the world, as was demonstrated by the multi-national attendees eager to take back the ways of the British Army to their native lands. But he was still unaccustomed to leading their rag-tag band in defensive infantry tactics without resupply or additional support. It felt unorthodox and more than a little desperate at times. As much as he hated to admit it to himself, the bonds of discipline and service were beginning to unravel everywhere he looked. Uniform wore out and was replaced by civilian clothing, and the cold weather diluted that compliance further still as the men wore whatever they could find to stop them from freezing, just as he did, but at least he still tried to maintain some semblance of protocol.

A knock at the door snapped him out of his miserable reverie, and he drew in a breath to announce that the person should enter, but he swallowed the word as the door opened a fraction of a second later; as though the knock was simply a warning instead of a request for permission. He relaxed when he saw who it was, leaning back and crossing his arms for warmth to tuck his cold hands under his armpits.

"Julian, how are you?" Lieutenant Lloyd asked.

"I'm well, thank you, Chris," Palmer answered with a genuine smile. He liked the Royal Marine officer, seeing in the slightly younger man a leader who was respected by his men, and capable.

Perhaps 'capable' is grossly inadequate, he had thought to himself when assessing the man, *as he is personally responsible for bringing the vast majority of our fighting strength out of the fiery hell that was the Island.*

And he was. It was his quick thinking and decisive action which had seen a ragged infantry formation, like a rally-square, which had crab-walked its awkward way up almost a mile of steep hill, fighting every step of the way and rescuing as many people as possible before forming a defence atop the hill. They had defended that landing site, suffering the agonising wait between the relay flights of the helicopter which had rescued them from the furnace.

Most of them, anyway.

"Going over the company books?" the junior officer asked blandly to open the conversation.

"Sadly yes," Palmer replied, "and they do not make for an enjoyable read, I'm afraid."

"Food?"

"Always food," Palmer replied tiredly. He glanced at the

crystal decanter, automatically feeling the urge to pour both of them a brandy as they discussed business, in spite of the time of day, but the vessel had long since run dry and as nobody had left the house in the weeks since the last attack, any hope of a fresh supply was woefully deluded.

"But also fuel; for the house and the vehicles. And we have burned through too much ammunition to make viable many more defensive actions of the nature we have already endured," he added in his naturally verbose manner, meaning simply that they were running out of bullets faster than they could afford to. His mind wandered to the strange trend he had witnessed emerging among both soldiers and civilians carrying crude melee weapons with them. Most soldiers relied on the bayonets affixed to the ends of their personal weapons, even if the destructive projectiles were in short supply, but many had also begun sporting folding shovels, hammers and small axes which stayed with them at all times.

"I think we need to discuss reconnaissance with the Major," he told the royal marine.

Lloyd nodded sagely as he sat, mulling over his friend's words. The roles and hierarchy of their group had merged and evolved too since their flight and devastating losses after the Island had become overrun and cut off, and as Palmer had been volunteered as the de-facto leader of the group, Lloyd had assumed a sub-command of the defences. Be they marine or trooper or civilian, everyone assigned to defend their home had fallen under the command of the Lieutenant without question or protest, bar one man. Palmer's younger brother, Oliver, who still insisted on using the double-barrelled version of their family name as though status and breeding meant a damn thing when abandoned and facing starvation, had been assigned to Lloyd as his second in command.

The junior Lieutenant was universally scorned and disliked by the men after his behaviour had once more grown sullen and smacked of assumed privilege. His older brother had hoped that to assign him to that task would make him more accessible to the men, and would allow them to see him working hard, but he too often heard that he was delegating his duties in favour of spending time rubbing shoulders with the half-insensible Colonel who provided little to no practical assistance in their plight. Palmer had managed to steal the senior officer's two privates away from the man to bolster the defenders' numbers, but Second Lieutenant Palmer's repeated absences from duty were both embarrassing and inconsequential.

"The Major will be pleased," Lloyd opined, "I think he and his boys are suffering from a little cabin fever."

The Major in question, Clive Downes, while clearly a more experienced and senior officer, had declined the gracious offer to lead their group, claiming that it wasn't his area of business. Palmer, as much as he hated the responsibility on a daily basis, had to agree. Having a four-man Special Air Service patrol at his disposal was something of a luxury when it came to stepping outside the relative safety of their draughty home. On every occasion they had planned to raid an area for supplies, he had first allowed the special forces soldiers to go in quietly and return to provide an in-depth intelligence report on enemy activity and the requirements of any ensuing mission. This template had worked flawlessly until the weather had turned, but the voluntary grounding of their helicopter in order to preserve the fuel and mechanical integrity of the aircraft had greatly limited their abilities. Now, he felt, necessity would force them to brave the treacherous weather in order to survive.

"I'll speak to him," Palmer said, "because I doubt we have more than two or three weeks' worth of food remaining, even on reduced rationing."

That seemed to end their conversation on that matter, as neither wanted to face the realities of their dire situation. That situation extended solely to food, luckily, as they still had running water for reasons unknown to them. They had power still, but they knew the cause for this was as a direct result of a mission carried out by the Major and his team back when there was still hope of containing the nationwide outbreak, and they were inserted by helicopter to a nuclear power plant, where the dial was effectively cranked back down to the lowest setting. The engineers had assured them that the plant would run for many more years like that, as it only needed the constant maintenance to run at optimal levels. Given that the demand for electricity was only a fraction of what it had been before, they hadn't experienced any loss of power. The power alone didn't help that they were all freezing slowly to death, however.

Very uncommonly for the area, their luck ran out when they dived headlong into the worst winter any of them could recall. The marines grumbled that they preferred their arctic warfare training in the Norwegian winter to the conditions they were facing now, because at least there they were prepared and equipped appropriately. His own men had even taken to wearing their NBC, or nuclear/biological/chemical, protection suits over their clothing, in an effort to block out the worst of the cold.

Lloyd put a stop to the grumbling of his marines before it gathered momentum by assembling his men and telling them all to reach down with their right hands to check that they still had balls, which silenced any further complaints.

The worst affected areas of the vast house, which was heated by log and coal fires and the precious heating oil which fired the huge Aga in the old part of the kitchen, had been granted the use of the gas-bottle powered heaters, but as they were now a finite resource and the high ceilings made most of the heat they provided a waste, they were used sparingly. Palmer had a huge list of priorities to attend to, and heating was among those at the top of the list. He wanted a wholesale coal dealer emptied, almost salivating at the thought of sitting beside a roaring fire and being warm for the first time in weeks, but he knew that warmth would be pointless without food.

No, he told himself as he and Lloyd lapsed into a brooding silence, *we need food and we need it now.*

TWO

They had every intention of resting for only a day or two after finding the safety of the abandoned village, following their fluke survival of a brutal helicopter crash, but as always, best laid plans often fell at the first hurdle.

Finding the house had been total happenstance and discovering that there were two young children living there was utterly miraculous to them all. The resilience and bravery of the young boy, Peter, had emerged slowly as he relaxed more around them to speak about his experiences.

The young girl, Amber, still hadn't spoken a word to any of the adults, although she occasionally whispered into Peter's ear. She did show signs of warming up to one of them, however, and the way she stared at their Norwegian parachute commando bordered on the obsessive at times.

Johnson, in a rare moment of giving in to the urge to smoke, took the packet scavenged from one of the village houses and a lighter to the back garden, and leaned back to perch on the low stone wall of the raised patio. As he lit the cigarette and inhaled, the sound of the sliding doors opening and closing made him turn awkwardly to crane his neck around the bulk of his right shoulder to see who it was. Surprised to see that it was Peter, he nodded to the boy, who zipped up his oversized coat all the way to his cheeks in response to the chill in the air, and came to rest on the frosty stone near to the man three times his size. The two sat in comfortable silence for a time, both staring out over the low ground which fell away from the rear of their modest castle at the thin wisps of mist hanging near to the frozen dew on the grass.

"She likes Astrid, doesn't she?" Johnson asked the boy, meaning to discern the reasons behind the little girl's stares at the blonde-haired commando. Peter sighed and dropped his head.

"Her mum had hair like she does," he answered simply. Johnson said nothing for a while, going back over the facts he had in his head about their story.

"What happened to her mother?" he asked gently, "You said you found her."

"I did," Peter said sadly, before pausing and explaining, "I was hiding in a house and heard people. In a car. They broke into another house and dragged her away, then they broke into the house I was hiding in, but they didn't find me. When they left, I went to look and I found Amber."

Johnson drew in a breath, fighting down the savage words that had loaded themselves on the tip of his tongue, ready to fire. He swallowed them down and thought before responding.

"You're a very brave young man, Peter," he said carefully, forcing the anger out of his voice in case the boy misunderstood and thought it was directed at him. He knew why men would drag away a woman, but he doubted that Peter would or even that he *should* understand that yet. "I wish I had a few dozen as brave as you in my squadron." Instantly he regretted

his words, as only one of the men who had served under him
had shown anything but the utmost effort and bravery. Those
men were gone now, scattered and dead to a man possibly, but
he had to hope that they had stayed together and stayed alive.

"I had to kill one of the monsters, though," Peter went on
as though Johnson hadn't spoken. "The front door was broken
and it just... walked in. Probably following the noise," he
added, with a sensibility and maturity beyond his small frame
and short years.

Johnson had no words this time, so he lowered his head
and smoked thoughtfully. His natural manner left him lost
when dealing with children; as though he didn't know how to
be around them after a lifetime of being ordered and giving
orders among other rough men. Instead he chose to change the
subject.

"You're up early," he said.

"Don't sleep much anymore," Peer said wistfully, his words
again making him sound decades older than he was, as though
the experience of the last few months had aged him beyond
repair and had ended his childhood years before it should have
faded into adulthood.

"Want to do the morning checks with me?" asked the
Squadron Sergeant Major without a squadron or any men to
command, taking a final drag and grinding out the cigarette
into the frozen ground. In response, Peter stood and nodded.

Johnson put on a woolly hat and picked up his tools, taking
one of the suppressed submachine guns from where the
weapons rested against the wall in the lounge. Peter took his
own weapon from that rack too, having taken to placing it
there to mimic the adults he idolised but didn't know how to
engage with comfortably. He always carried the small spike,
like a crude and homemade ice pick, and he slipped the sawn-
off shotgun into his small backpack as he hefted the pitchfork

and looked up to Johnson, nodding to signify that he was ready to go.

Johnson checked that his gun was loaded, which he knew it always would be, and slung it behind him to pick up what had become his primary weapon in the form of a small sledgehammer. Most men would tire even carrying such a tool, let alone have the strength to swing it more than a few times to crush the skulls of former human beings, but Johnson managed it.

They hadn't been forced to do much in the way of fighting since they had arrived there, especially seeing as Peter had dispatched a tenth of the undead still trapped inside the small village before their appearance, but when the injuries to Kimberley and the irascible Sergeant Hampton had taken longer than expected to heal and allow them mobility, they had decided to stay where they were until their entire contingent was fully fit. Johnson had told them about the plan to form up at the base and search for another permanent site after that, but their early foray to that base had been met with depressing evidence of carnage and destruction. Of the three sites suggested for the squadron to reform, Johnson could not recall any of the locations, so had spent days on end compiling a list of potential sites to be checked for their companions, if any yet survived. Shortly after they had found the village, a helicopter had been heard, but when they went outside into the secluded back garden to check, the aircraft had disappeared and had not been seen since. In case it came back over, Johnson had found a large tub of white gloss paint and used a broom to push the sticky white fluid around on the empty patch of road by the house. He painted four simple characters, not writing 'help', but instead leaving his individual calling card in his radio callsign. If whatever was flying around was military, which it almost certainly had to be, then seeing the legend of F33A emblazoned on the road below, *Foxtrot-Three-Three-Alpha*, would grab their attention instantly.

Before they knew it, however, and far sooner than they had expected, the temperatures had dropped and the first snow fell to entomb them for over a week and obscure their aerial message. After that, the priority to move and take their uncertain chances on the road fell into second place behind surviving the winter.

Holding the big hammer in one hand and turning to the only other person in the house who was awake, he announced where they were going.

"Doing the lap," he said to Enfield, the oddly quiet and calm sniper filling the kettle for the first brew of the day, who simply nodded in response. Johnson paid no attention to what would have previously, in their old lives, earned the young marine an arse-chewing of epic proportions for failing to correctly acknowledge a warrant officer of his standing and position, regardless of them being from different branches of the armed forces. Johnson was never a man to enforce such displays of obedience, he had never needed to as his men respected him, and he didn't feel the slightest need to do so now. Even less so given that the majority of their small force were either current or former royal marines. He knew that Enfield meant no disrespect by the gesture, far from it in fact, but the man wasn't in the habit of wasting unnecessary words when a silent look or a nod would suffice.

Doing the lap was what they called their morning routine of patrolling the perimeter of the small village which had been cleared and fortified during the weeks they had been there. Vehicles had been used to block access through their home, rolled and pushed into position before being jacked up and having their wheels removed to prevent them being pushed back out of position just as easily. In between every gap they had piled the furniture taken from the houses, leaving a single space blocked by two vehicles which could be moved should they need to drive their chosen transport out, which they hadn't done for weeks, given the driving rain and sharp frosts in between the intermittent flurries of snow.

On the outside of those barricades were as many sharpened fence posts and other obstacles designed to snag any unsuspecting dead to wander in their direction as could be sharpened and emplaced. The rear of the dozen houses in the village, which been cleared of anything useful, had been reinforced similarly with coils of fencing found nearby to tangle anything walking in across country. The only other building in the small village not to have been hollowed out was the small pub at the slightly higher elevated end of the tiny strip, which was really little more than a long, low room containing a bar, a fireplace and a selection of dark wood tables and chairs with a dartboard adorning one wall and innumerable stains of suspect origin. That space was left as a kind of retreat; a place where any of them could fall back to and work through their own thoughts, which they found that they needed to do with increasing frequency, given their enforced lack of activity to occupy their minds.

The resources found in the village, the canned food and dried goods looted from all the other houses, had kept them fed for enough time to regain their strength, but occasionally they had been forced to venture out to nearby places for more until their immediate surroundings had been stripped bare.

As Johnson and the small boy whose shoulders reached not much above the man's waist walked the lap, checking each section for any sign of life or, more importantly, *former* life, he thought about the worries afflicting him.

How long can we last, living like this? What kind of existence is it, especially for the young ones? What happens when we run out of ammo, or the baffles on the suppressed weapons finally give up, or we can no longer get a vehicle to start?

He tried to answer his own questions, realising that he no idea how to respond to each one without raising yet more questions about the answers he'd conjured up. He knew that they needed a plan, needed so much more than they had in so many ways, but other than taking them all on the road, he had no idea what to do. They had power and heat in the form of the electrically powered fan heaters. They even had a limited supply of hot water thanks to the solar panels on the south-facing slope of the roof they lived under, which never truly got that hot given the current weather. But they were relatively safe, they weren't suffering too badly from the elements, and they weren't starving. Yet.

"There's one," Peter said softly, snapping him out of his thoughts. Johnson looked down at the boy, followed his gaze past his outstretched finger to see an immobile body slumped over the front of a dark blue Ford saloon car.

"What's the difference between an Orion and an Escort from the front?" he asked himself out loud. Peter made a small noise of confusion and prompted the man to shake himself out of his distraction.

Johnson put a large, flat palm out in front of Peter, indicating that he should stay back, but not touching him. The thing posed no risk to them as it was, not unless they were foolish enough to put themselves within biting distance and wait for it to wake up.

That was one of the strangest things to have happened, just one development in a very extensive list, but they still found themselves shocked at new developments. The cold seemed to affect the Screechers, seemed to slow them and make them sluggish, but it also seemed to accelerate the way they rotted and fell apart. Already they had discovered a big change in the ones they unearthed from inside houses; the musty smelling ones that were more preserved than others. The unlucky ones who had found themselves outside fared much worse due to exposure to the elements; to the constant rain and freezing temperatures of the harsh early winter, which made their flesh wither and often fall way in chunks. Their skin became something in between grey and clear, hanging from them in landslides of saggy flesh, and resembled the bloated corpses one might expect to see dragged from the River Thames after being missing for three weeks. Their movements were halting and uncoordinated and often they would be inexplicably missing fingers, which he guessed had frozen solid and snapped off. This one didn't perk up, nor did it respond to their approach as they continued to check the section of the perimeter between their position and the trapped Screecher.

When they did approach, Johnson again gesturing for Peter to stay back, the long and knotted hair twitched as the head rose to slowly rotate on an angle until the clouded, milky orbs locked onto the SSM. He hefted his hammer, leaning over the frosty car to judge the swing required to brain it, when he lost his footing slightly. The woman, almost naked and not looking remotely good, as her withered and sagging breasts slapped softly against her emaciated ribcage, sparked up and clawed a hand at him as it animated close to the level resembling their unexcited state in warmer weather. Johnson recoiled, calling the woman a few choice names as he decided to approach the problem differently. He climbed over the next vehicle along, jumped down on the far side, having first to push out to clear the spikes so he could land unimpeded.

As his boots hit the floor, he slipped on the icy surface, feeling the slight crunch of one ankle as he tried and failed to roll in an imitation of a parachute landing, and he sprawled out to feel his hammer slip out of his grip. He opened his eyes after he landed hard to watch it slide ahead of him and skitter to a stop just out of reach. A hoarse croak, high-pitched and hissing, sounded from behind him, as if the thing impaled against the car was trying to screech, as was their horrifying way, but had lost its voice. He turned in dread, seeing that it had pushed, pulled and fallen away from the sharpened wood it had been stuck against to land on the pitted road surface beside his boots.

He pedalled his feet frantically, desperate for purchase to propel him away from the thing, and as his hands fumbled for the weapon trapped under his back, he heard a single word ring out.

"Oi," it said, the voice unbroken but as confident as any soldier he had ever served with.

The sound that followed the voice was a metallic singing, culminating in a crunch and the solid noise of Peter's pitchfork hitting the tarmac on the other side of the skull he had just skewered. The hissing and huffing of the thing had stopped in the same instant, and Johnson followed the line of the metal sprouting from the inanimate head, back up the worn wooden handle and past the boy's hands to his face, which held no sign of humour or pride or expectation.

"You alright?" he asked the SSM.

"Yeah," Johnson said in shock, startled and feeling cold to his core at how quickly a slight mistake could change, or *end*, a person's life, "Ankle's tweaked," he said, the feeling in his body returning as the adrenaline ebbed away and the pain rushed in to replace it.

"It's icy," Peter told him as he jerked the spike back out of the skull. Johnson bit back the sarcastic retort that he was well aware of that salient fact and thank you very much for pointing it out all the same. He regained his feet as the boy was cleaning the weapon on the shredded and torn remains of the clothes his victim still wore, hissing in discomfort as he put pressure on the joint but retrieving his sledgehammer and dragging the lightweight corpse away from the road to roll it on the grass before limping slightly back to regain the safer side of their barricade. He hadn't even seen Peter get over to save him, hadn't heard the boy move until he had dealt the fatal blow, and he rather suspected that a platoon of Peters would be worth putting money on at decent odds.

"Let's keep that bit to ourselves, shall we?" he asked the boy as they walked back to complete their lap. Peter only smiled in answer.

THREE

"Understood," Downes said simply when Palmer told him what was on his mind.

A man with less style, less impeccably honed manners, would have found such a conversation awkward. Julian Palmer, with his natural aristocratic charm, possessed that effortless way of making a polite suggestion in conversation, or merely presenting a problem to someone so that they volunteered to undertake the solution, instead of having to give an order. In that sense he reminded himself of their former Sergeant Major, the very heart of the squadron in many ways, as he too rarely had to give an order; merely a suggestion that men jumped to carry out.

"I'll need a decent vehicle capable of dealing with all of this," Downs said, waving a vague hand over the outside air to encompass the weather in general.

"Done," Palmer said, his mind calculating the available vehicles and fuel supplies remaining and settling on the four-year-old Toyota Land Cruiser found on the nearby farm. A good choice, given that their own military vehicles were both unfamiliar to the SAS men and notoriously unreliable, especially after the months of abuse they had suffered with little to no maintenance.

"And it's likely to take a couple of days," Downes added, "I'll have Mac draw up a comms schedule and get the boys looking at the maps again."

"You have my thanks, Major," Palmer said humbly, taking his leave to return to the more mundane matters.

On his walk back to the room he had adopted as an office, he took the long way around via the large, grassed inner court-yard to view the half-ploughed lawns where the vegetable planting had been planned but started too late in the autumn, before the ground froze hard, and which still showed no signs of thawing. They had grossly miscalculated how long their stores of food would last, burning through the ration packs at a rate not quite as desperate as their remaining ammunition, but still too fast to make surviving winter a foregone conclusion. They needed more food, they needed more fuel for fires, and they needed it now.

He had thought ahead in the last week, diverting men from the former Headquarters Troop to join his only remaining radio operator, Corporal Daniels, in a room which had become their unofficial command. There they studied maps of the area, sadly being more topographical than detailed as to the contents of each town and village, and they scanned the lists of the local directory to find businesses that could be of help to their plight. Palmer's own small office, what he had guessed had been the snug belonging to the former master of the house, was only a door away and he often found himself working alongside the men, instead of spiralling into depres-sion when left alone with his thoughts.

Hindsight, he told himself sourly, *is a wonderful thing. We should have started planting food as soon as we got to this place. Should have used the remainder of the good weather to search for more. So many things we should have done.*

But they hadn't done these things. *He* hadn't. They had all rested on their small laurels and enjoyed the relative safety and relaxation, and now they had to survive somehow until the weather broke, which he knew could be half a year away. The thought of huddling in the cold and living on little to no food for all that time threatened to push him further into the depressive cycle he felt himself swirling around, and he knew that if *he* felt that way, then others were certain to feel the same or worse. That brought with it other concerns, and he worried that the discipline of the civilians, as well as his own adopted men, would begin to unravel.

An early stroke of luck was finding that the nearby farm, accessible either by a cross-country walk of almost a mile or a three-mile journey by single-track roads, possessed a pair of greenhouses which had provided tomatoes and cucumbers for two weeks before they ran out. After that, they had been forced to try and remedy their sudden lack of fresh food, and plant more of it. Crops of onions and carrots had been planted, along with spring onions, broad beans and peas, but they were slow to grow in the sudden low temperatures and the yield was far too small to be worthwhile. What they did manage was large batches of stews, which were started by the volunteer contingent of civilians each morning, and which cooked throughout the day in huge metal pots on the Aga. Then when the sun began to set, everyone ate in shifts.

Work teams toiled all day, clearing rooms and arranging things as best they could for comfort. Men and women walked over the low hill to the farm where they took everything of use, which had blessedly included some livestock that still lived. A large and docile horse had been brought inside to be stabled for winter, as had half a dozen cows, which one of the women rescued from the Island knew how to milk by hand. The farm was more of a smallholding and not a large commercial one, and the occupants had left in such a hurry that their livestock had been abandoned. There were chickens and pigs too, but the eagerness of the survivors on finding them had decimated the herds and flocks before Palmer had ordered men to guard the farm, and had spread the word to keep every animal alive. The simple logic of a daily dose of protein in the form of an egg being more important to their survival than a single roast chicken, needed explaining in detail, it seemed, which infuriated the young officer.

The remaining chickens, safe for now from hungry mouths, laid a modest batch of eggs every day, which, just as the fresh vegetables, was nowhere near enough for all of them. He needed to supplement, to think for all of them, and he did so in every way that he could. He spread the word throughout the civilians as he did the military men, asking for experience in trapping game. Soon he had a team of three men who went out each night and each morning to set and check the snares for rabbit and hare, which were more abundant in the area than he had ever noticed before.

Throughout the brief end of summer and early autumn, those snares had been constantly pilfered by the few Screechers roaming the countryside aimlessly, but as the temperature dropped, so too did the numbers of wandering dead they encountered. The snares provided a meagre supply of meat which found its way into the stews, every shred of flesh stripped from the bones in acceptable mimicry of their enemy.

He hadn't taken the time to consider this perceived disappearance of Screechers, nor did he really have that time available, but when he tried to find slumber, that was one of the innumerable questions that kept him from sleep. The reduction in numbers of flesh-eating undead human beings was a blessing, and most people considered it as simply that, but he refused to accept the assumptions that they were moving off or dying out. He kept his men alert, planned exercises with the other officers and NCOs to rouse the men and women from their sleep, as though they were under attack again. He had done this only twice since they had been attacked in force, both times feeling barely satisfied with the response times, but he'd chosen not to do so again as the backlash from the civilians was unbearable; they were unaccustomed to that kind of life, couldn't cope emotionally or physically with being woken up in the night to react and then told to go back to sleep, because they weren't soldiers.

"What have we got, boys?" he announced cheerily as he walked into the room containing men bent over maps, wearing a smile that his eyes could not hope to match.

"The coal place seems viable, Sir," answered Trooper Cooper who had been made acting Sergeant Cooper as the only remaining man in the HQ Troop seeming to possess more than a few braincells, "and there's a few supermarkets a bit further out that would be a good idea, only they're closer to the towns," he finished, a gentle warning in his tone.

Palmer nodded, knowing that sending men into the larger towns near the coast could be catastrophic.

"The Hereford lot are getting ready to go out," he said, "get everything you can on your top three supply sites to me as soon as possible, if you please."

"Sir," Cooper responded curtly, his single word conveying compliance and not annoyance. Palmer nodded to them and left, walking back out into the long, carpeted walkway where he almost collided with Maxwell.

"Shit me! Sorry, Sir," he said from behind two large sacks rested on his right shoulder. Maxwell had adopted the role of senior NCO, performing well in the shadow of the loss of Johnson, who was mourned and muttered about by many.

"Not to worry, Mister Maxwell," Palmer answered as he stepped back, using the honorary address as he would a sergeant major, despite the man still wearing the three chevrons of his actual rank, "but please do tell me what you have there."

"Flour, Sir," Maxwell answered almost excitedly as he rummaged with his free hand in the pocket of his smock to produce a large, rustling plastic packet, "and yeast!"

Palmer stared at him, his mouth slightly open, which Maxwell took to be a lack of comprehension.

"I'm taking it to the kitchens," he said, "I'll ask Denise to make some fresh bread for tonight's stew. She just needs a little salt and a bit of oil, see, and you knead it together, then rest it to let it rise, th…"

"I'm aware of the process, Maxwell," Palmer interrupted him, unsure how he even knew, given that his family home was graced with a cook and staff, "I was more concerned with where you found it."

"Farmhouse, Sir, tucked away in a shed," he replied, falling back on the senior NCO style of giving loud, crisp and punctilious answers when dealing with officers. Palmer knew and recognised the routine immediately, abandoning any further line of questioning as pointless.

"Well, my compliments to Mrs Maxwell," he said formally, "and I'll expect a nice, fresh crust with the evening meal."

"Very good, Sir," Maxwell answered, resuming his burdened march towards the kitchen. Palmer watched him go, thoughts bouncing around his head until his gurgling stomach changed the subject for him. Clasping an involuntary hand to his thinning midsection, he lost his train of thought for a moment and returned to the office where the planning had happened.

"Village bakeries," he announced gleefully to the room, earning uncomprehending stares from four sets of eyes.

"Sir?" Cooper asked, his face asking the question far more than the inflection did.

"Tactically, it's wiser to avoid the more built-up areas, correct?" he asked rhetorically, but seeing that Cooper opened his mouth to respond, he continued quickly, "but the smaller villages are all but abandoned, or at least the Screechers there are contained," he paused, waiting to see if any of them had cottoned on to his idea yet. They hadn't.

"We go into the small bakers' and grocers'" he went on enthusiastically, "and take their flour and yeast and salt... they will have all the ingredients to bake bread, surely, so we bring that back and add fresh bread to the menu. I can't believe..."

His stomach growled audibly again, silencing his enthusiastic speech and raising the eyebrows of the other men in the room.

"Here you go, Sir," Daniels said in an almost embarrassed tone, reaching into a pouch and coming out with the remnant of a shiny green wrapper, "have a dead fly biscuit before you drop."

Palmer smiled, gratefully accepting the gesture and the hard biscuit laced with dried fruit, as he knew the men well enough to not feel embarrassed by breaking down the divide between officer and troopers a level. As he chewed, his stomach protested again as it eagerly accepted the food, but Daniels wasn't finished.

"Oi, Coops, give the Captain one of them Rolos you're hiding."

Cooper looked shocked, maybe even a little hurt, and his mouth hung open to begin a feeble protest before the corporal cut him off.

"Don't pretend you ain't got any," Daniels said with a rueful smile, "we've all seen you. Peel a bloody orange in his pocket, that bugger would, Sir."

Cooper deflated before he spoke.

"It's my last one though," he admitted feebly, sparking laughter among the others.

"Aw, Coops," Daniels chuckled, "don't you love the Captain enough to give him your last Rolo?"

Amidst the laughter at his expense, Cooper reached into his

clothing and brought out a tangle of paper and foil wrapping which contained a solitary, lonely, chocolate-covered treat.

"It's quite alright, Sergeant," Palmer said, playing along, "I wouldn't want you to display such affection in front of your peers and cause unnecessary embarrassment." He let the laughter die down, chewing the hard biscuit and feeling better for it, before reiterating his orders.

"All of the local bakeries, if you would?" he said, his slightly full mouth betraying how much his hunger overrode his breeding, "and I'll speak to Lieutenant Lloyd to request a detachment of his men to get straight on it. The other task still stands."

He kicked himself for not thinking of this before, only forming the idea when he saw Maxwell carrying the sack of flour. He had so many demands on his time and energies that he was missing the answers directly in front of his face, and those demands seemed to grow every day. That list of problems requiring solutions and action grew, boiled over, and almost caused a fire in an instant, with the outbreak of pure pandemonium from down the hallway outside his office.

FOUR

"Jesus, it's cold," Nevin complained as he blew on his hands and rubbed them, before holding them over the fire he was crouching in front of.

"It's winter," Michaels answered with an undisguised lack of interest, "it happens."

Nevin ignored the sarcastic retort as he stared into the flames, his face contorting into a rictus of distaste for the man he had been forced to bow and scrape to over the weeks since he had joined the group on the Hilltop. At first the grass had been very green, with stockpiles of looted beer and spirits and good cigarettes, which were a luxury to him. Once that initial hangover had passed, made worse by that bastard Johnson limiting them to a single pint a day for his own amusement, he had realised that the utopia he had imagined wasn't a reality.

It could be, he told himself in quiet moments, *but not with Michaels at the helm.*

The surprise of finding their squadron's missing troop sergeant had stayed with him for over a week, until he realised that the man he had known before wasn't the man he spoke with now. Sergeant Michaels had been a quiet man, fastidious in some respects, and hard on his men, but ultimately committed to them and rewarding when the appropriate time came. The man sitting in the ornate chair behind him in the grand parlour was still quiet, but there seemed to be an element to him now that was either lacking something he had possessed before, or else there was an edge he had gained since. Nevin mused that it could be both; that the loss of family and the addition of lawlessness had changed the man, much as it had changed him.

On balance, he much preferred the Hilltop way of life, in that he was never roused from an uncomfortable sleep to sit and keep watch with the promise of punishment if he didn't perform his duties under the malevolent watch of senior men. Senior in their eyes, at least, but not in Nevin's. He had shed the uniform as soon as he'd arrived, and bundled the dirty clothing stained with sweat, blood and the acrid stench of dried urine, handing them to a cowed woman to be washed and ironed. He had wanted to burn the uniform, but Michaels had insisted that he keep it ready. The rationale for that insistence, as much as Nevin didn't understand it at first, became evident when they had visited a group of nearby settlers who had found themselves in a similarly protected position as the Hilltop.

The rolling higher ground near the seaside cliffs formed a natural barrier against the legions of undead who roamed across the countryside in the late summer, making those on the lower ground inland vulnerable. The unmistakable sounds of battle in the previous months had tugged at Michaels' thoughts until Nevin had been thoroughly questioned about the two actions to defend the island, and those facts had further solidified his gut feelings about the lower ground.

That geography, nature's defences, had protected dozens of

small pockets of humanity along the coast, and the arrival of Nevin provided Michaels with the additional tool he required to make further acquisitions.

Dressed in his uniform, Nevin was inspected by the former sergeant who wore nothing to indicate the life he had abandoned, other than the webbing and weapons taken from the camp. Michaels instructed Nevin very precisely in what to say and do, and after sunrise he rolled out at the head of a small convoy in the Ferret car he had taken from the camp before he had abandoned the rest of his squadron to die by flame, explosion or the teeth and nails of the dead. The other vehicles, a collection of civilian cars and vans driven by the cruel followers of Michaels and his litter of lawlessness, dropped back to wait out of sight of the big farm, as Nevin powered up the chalk stone track to the fenced enclave, where he was met by three men holding shotguns unthreateningly.

"Good morning," he exclaimed from the hatch, in an accent designed to mimic any number of officers he had soldiered under, "we're conducting reconnaissance of the area," he explained without introduction, "and are collecting numbers and dispositions of survivors."

His arrogance served him well, as Michaels had explained that people would long for someone in authority to arrive and give them instructions. That assumed authority, which he had to admit to himself that he enjoyed, instantly put the men at ease and prompted the emergence of women and a few children from the front door of the farmhouse. Nevin asked them questions, receiving freely given answers in the naïve belief that the man represented the armed forces instead of a band of pirates. He had climbed out of the scout car, shaking hands with the men and giving broad smiles to the others, who relaxed the more he spoke.

When he had gleaned as much information as his orders

had dictated, hearing about how proud they were to still be producing their own milk and meat and vegetables, and still smiling as he did it, he produced the revolver and shot the oldest man holding a gun through the fleshy part of his lower leg.

He felt nothing as he did it. His smile didn't falter or fade as he showed no remorse for his actions and the taking of a life. He'd become numb to death and pain and suffering, seeing it as a natural course of action as much as breathing was, because this was now the way of the world for him.

The other armed men reacted amidst the screams and shouts of their friends, until a brief, deafening rip of thirty-calibre bullets tore the air and silenced them all. Despite himself and the knowledge of what would happen, Nevin still flinched instinctively from the noise, until he straightened once more in the renewed silence, to smile at the terrified huddle of men, women and children.

The turret on the scout car rotated audibly, swinging down to aim at the group in unspoken threat.

"Now listen to me," Nevin snarled over the sobs, "you lot will give up food for us to take away, and we expect the same every month. That," he said, pointing the barrel of his revolver at the old man who was bleeding and crying onto the frosted stones of the courtyard amidst the desperate attention of the women, "is your one and *only* warning about what will happen if you don't do as you are told."

He stayed silent, staring them down and knowing that Michaels would be watching and listening from his position behind the controls of the heavy machine gun. The sounds of multiple engines behind him as the rest of their convoy approached up the track, filled him with yet more confidence in his power over people.

"We don't want to kill all of you, and we don't want to

drive you off. All we want is a bit of what you have, and we'll keep you safe in return. Now," he said as he indicated the shot man again, "strap that up and keep it clean. It'll heal in time."

And that was effectively their game. They ran a criminal protection racket. Their process and tactics had evolved with the arrival of Nevin and the heavy gun he'd brought with him, and Michaels was grateful for the addition of another trained man to provide some spine to the collection of men and women who followed him, because a life spent taking when contrasted to a life spent providing was the easier route to take. He could easily have roamed the landscape in the Warrior he'd taken, but his preference was to retain that for defence of a permanent position, because that made him feel more secure. He hid his insecurities well, as outwardly he was every inch the cold, hard man he projected.

They loaded the cars with milk, meat, vegetables and eggs, taking much more than the remaining survivors could afford to give and still live as comfortably as they had done, and they took it all back to the Hilltop, where the approach road was overlooked by the half-buried hulk of the Warrior light tank that Michaels had emplaced when he had arrived there. Nevin abandoned the uniform, dropping it on the floor, knowing that the lesser people would pick it up and fold it ready for their next rouse. Then, not to waste the daylight, he dressed in a leather coat over jeans and boots to go back out.

Michaels' reason for subduing the farm had been to prevent them from seeing his people passing by on the road below them, as there were resources in the next town that needed more firepower to take. He rode with Nevin, the controls of the machine gun feeling good in his hands as they rolled ahead of the soft-skinned and vulnerable vehicles behind.

"We couldn't take this place before," he said into the

headset he wore that linked him to Nevin and allowed them to communicate over the din of the engine, "not without the risk of losing too many people anyway. There was some kind of community aid station set up in the town, and there are probably a hundred of the things in between us and what we want."

"And what do we want?" Nevin asked out of curiosity but lacking the interest to know the minutia of a plan.

"Food," Michaels said, "there's a Bejam's there which still has lights on, so the freezers should still be working too."

"You mean Iceland?" Nevin asked, knowing that the shop had been bought out and rebranded, and choosing to allow his natural tendency of nit picking to emerge.

"Whatever," Michaels said, uninterested, "there's a gun shop and a tool place there as well. I want those."

Nevin didn't answer. He didn't overly care, as he was just happy to be served and fed and to force others to bend to his will. They retraced their route and rolled into the outskirts of the town, passing by the unmarked entrance leading up to the farm, where doubtless the people there would be tending to their loved one and reeling from the after effects of Nevin's actions.

"Stop by that junction," Michaels instructed, steadying himself as Nevin slowed sharply, "that building there, red double-doors."

"Yeah?"

"Get out and open them," Michaels instructed him blankly. Nevin's face set in a look of anger and disgust, deciding against upsetting the man who would be aiming a destructive gun at his back, and he popped open the hatch to climb out. He ran towards the building, eyes scanning wildly left and right as he went, reaching the doors and steadying himself with a few breaths before spinning the handles and wrenching them both open with a grunt and preparing for an onslaught of dead rushing him.

None came, surprising him until the stench hit him in the face with as much recalled force as Johnson's large fist. Regaining his senses, he ran hard back for the safety of the Ferret and scrambled inside to pull down the hatch, just as the gun opened up over his head in short, controlled bursts which spoke of a calmness and discipline few possessed.

FIVE

Not wanting to waste the day, given that it was just cold and not raining or hailing or snowing, as it had been intermittently throughout the week, Johnson removed his right boot and applied a bandage with difficulty to the aggravated joint. As he was struggling to do it, Astrid walked in and tutted loudly.

"This is why men cannot wrap the gifts," she announced cryptically, snapping her fingers and reaching out for the bandage. Johnson abandoned the task, leaning back on the sofa with a huff as he handed it over.

"You made a twist of it? How?" she asked him as she knelt on the expensive rug at his feet and rolled the bandage back up to begin again.

"Slipped on the ice," he admitted, leaving out the relevant information that the simple accident would almost certainly have spelled disaster, had it not been for the ten-year-old boy saving his life.

"You should be more careful," Astrid admonished him gently, her tone indicating that she might have already known or guessed the facts that he hadn't stated, "especially at your age."

"My *age*?" Johnson asked, carefully enunciating the words with an edge of warning.

"Yes," she said, unperturbed by his tone, "I simply mean that you do not heal as quickly as you would have done when you were younger. A sprain of the ankle could make the differences of life and death, but luckily this is not swollen."

"Thanks," Johnson said, feeling the practised hands of the woman wrapping the bandage far more effectively around his sore joint, but further discussion was cut off by Buffs walking into the room and shrugging into his equipment.

"You good to go?" he asked, eyeing the treatment happening in their living room.

"I am," Johnson answered with finality.

"Good. Me, you, Astrid and Craig," he said, detailing their team to go out. It made sense, as Hampton was still struggling to put his full weight on the knee that he had dislocated in the helicopter crash. Kimberley was healed and mobile, but being unfamiliar with firearms, she wasn't the obvious choice to take, plus any more bodies on their foray would reduce the quantity of supplies they could return with and increase the risk of discovery.

"Can I come?" asked a small voice from the open-plan kitchen behind them, forcing Johnson to twist to see Peter's hopeful expression. He took in the look on his face, turning back to Buffs in the hope that he would dash the boy's hopes.

"I don't take up much room," he added, melting the hearts of the hard men just a little.

"I know, lad," Buffs said softly, "but with Bill still slow as a snail, who is here to keep the village safe? Who's going to protect Kimberley and Amber?"

Peter, his hopes of joining the elite dashed in such a way as to elevate his mood, gave a resolved smile and nodded, accepting the refusal with grace and purpose, as he accepted the promotion solemnly.

"You look after this place," Johnson added, "and we'll see if we can bring you something good back, shall we?"

"Like what?" Peter asked, half in hope and half in suspicion, as he was woefully unaccustomed to adults showing him any kindness.

"What would you like? Some video cassettes? Books?" Astrid asked, fixing the bandage with a strip of black electrical tape taken from one of her pouches, and standing to allow Johnson the room to put his boot back on and lace it tightly.

Peter opened his mouth to speak but stopped as a small hand tugged at his sleeve. He bent down to Amber, knowing that she wouldn't speak out loud in front of everyone, and listened as she whispered in his ear insistently.

He smiled, straightened, and answered.

"Some new videos would be nice," he said, "and Amber wants a Kinder Surprise."

———

They took their van, the most appropriate vehicle found in the village for their needs, and carefully replaced the barrier of cars after they had moved outside their barricades. There were three seats across the front, and Johnson drove with Astrid beside him leaning her legs awkwardly into Bufford's to allow the SSM room to manipulate the gear stick without intruding on her intimately. Enfield rode in the back, uncomplaining, as riding in the front would have meant separating him from his rifle, because there just wouldn't have been enough space for both him and his gun.

Hampton had offered an opinion about that very subject, saying the loss of a long rifle in the man's hands was akin to severing a favoured male appendage. But it was also a tactical choice to sit in the back, as Enfield was the only one of them not to be carrying a suppressed weapon, should they need to get out and lay down fire in a hurry.

They drove carefully and slowly, aware of the treacherous road conditions, to keep their noise profile as low as possible, as was their standard operating procedure. They passed through small knots of buildings, some larger and others smaller than their own meagre stronghold, and past the combined post office and local shop that they had already emptied of anything useable. Twenty-five minutes of slow progress led them to the outer edge of a small town which bore the tell-tale signs of a swarm passing through. Only Johnson and Bufford had encountered the mass-gatherings of dead when they swarmed in impossible numbers, and neither wanted the experience repeated in a hurry. The shattered glass, the smears of gore and the shunted vehicles indicating an unstoppable tide of flesh passing through to clear the area of humanity like a plague, all indicated that something very unwelcome had befallen the town.

With the engine killed and ticking in the frosty silence, the four of them quietly got out and pushed the doors shut with as little sound as humanly possible. They fanned out, their drills wordless and smooth now as the four had learned to operate together more closely through practice, as Bufford led them towards their secondary objective, which was the closer of the two.

Approaching the glass frontage of the gun shop, they saw cracks spider-webbing from half a dozen impacts at head height, where they imagined the undead skulls of zombies had banged hard into the shop windows, which stood intact before the metal mesh grids inside. The door was unlocked, the shop largely untouched and showing no signs of having been ransacked. Gaps on the displays showed where guns had been removed in a hurry, but the locked cabinets of rifles remained intact.

Buffs and Astrid moved through the store, heading around the dark wooden counter and into the back, from where they returned almost instantly to declare the place empty. It only had a back storeroom filled with gun cabinets and a large lock-box like a chest freezer, a single toilet and a kitchen area, where no Screechers could be hidden. Grabbing three large game bags originally designed to hold the carcasses of animals from hunting trips, they set to work taking the heavy-load cartridges from the lock-box, which had yielded easily to Bufford's crow-bar. Astrid had turned to protect the front door as the other three began searching the shop.

"Any more rounds for your rifle?" Buffs asked Enfield, who looked up to meet his gaze.

"Three-oh-eights at a pinch," he said with a slight sneer at the thought of using inferior tools for his trade, "but they won't be as accurate over distance."

Johnson, who was stacking boxes of twelve-bore cartridges on the counter, the boxes bearing the lowest numbers to hand to indicate heavier shot, didn't think that accuracy over the distances their sniper was considering meant a great deal. He looked at him to voice that opinion, but saw the man heading across the shop floor towards a rack of rifles, with his head canted to the side as he zeroed in on the inspection.

Reaching up, Enfield lifted down a large gun with a dark wood stock that looked almost black. The huge optic seated over the barrel seemed fitting for the size of it, and he paused in his task to watch the quiet man turn it over in his hands and assess it almost lovingly. He hefted it, feeling the weight and balance and evidently finding it to his approval, then ran his hands tenderly over the bolt action a few times to find it smooth and well-machined. Dropping out the small magazine and reseating it, he nodded, looking around for a padded slip and placing the gun inside. Johnson went to turn back to his task, but clearly Enfield was not finished. Reaching up again, he took down a small, light weapon with bluey-grey metal on the barrel and trigger housing, with a deep, rich walnut stock. He pulled back the charging handle, making the clicking metallic sounds of a lighter, higher note than the more serious weapon he had held previously, and ran his hands over it in much the same way, before announcing over his shoulder what he needed.

"Two-two rimfire rounds," he said with purpose as he snapped his fingers excitedly, "as many as you can find."

Buffs paused in his search, meeting Johnson's eye before both men shrugged and began searching the lock-box for the requested bullets.

After ten minutes in the shop, piling up everything they wanted near Astrid by the door, Enfield was equipped with what he considered to be a barely suitable replacement for his Accuracy International when the military ammunition finally ran out, as well as a new personal weapon which seemed woefully small in comparison.

The small Ruger rifle, light and short-barrelled like a toy gun at a fairground sported a fat protrusion at the end of its length which none of them needed an explanation for. The sound baffle would doubtless reduce the noise of any shot, but they all knew that nothing was truly silent when it fired a bullet, as their own MP5s demonstrated with the snapping, chattering coughs they emitted. What Enfield knew but the others had yet to fathom was that the smaller calibre rifle wouldn't produce the tell-tale crack of high-velocity rounds as their other guns would. To him, it was the perfect Screecher killer.

Beside those chosen guns were box upon box of bullets and empty, spare magazines, next to the bags of shotgun cartridges capable of decapitating a person with ease. They helped themselves to other items after the priority of their resupply, taking thick hunting coats and waxed jackets. Johnson ran his hands quickly along the rack containing the smaller items before asking a question of the others in a low voice.

"How old is Amber, do you think?"

"Three? Four?" Bufford responded with a shrug, knowing about as much about children as Johnson did.

"She is not yet five," Astrid answered in her curious translation without taking her concentration away from the door. Johnson turned back to the rack and took two padded, waterproof coats in sizes ten and five, determined to provide for their youngest members.

"This is the last of the two-twos," Enfield said as he returned from the storeroom, bobbing his head and waving his hand over the stacked boxes as he did the mental calculations and finished with a hint of a smile, "Has anyone seen any keys?"

None of them had, meaning that whatever treasures lay locked away in the cabinets in the back would remain hidden. That was a shame for Enfield, who was something of a firearms connoisseur, especially in the light of recent changes to the UK gun laws which had prohibited some very useful items.

A little over two years before, they had learned of one of the worst losses of life at the hands of a civilian in their country. A man had killed sixteen people and critically injured almost as many, before taking his own life to take the count to seventeen dead. That had brought about massive change in the legal ownership of guns and had prohibited some semi-automatic rifles, as well as the ownership of handguns and shotguns able to fire more than three shots. That tragedy, that horrific loss of life, still somehow seemed worse in their memories than the unfathomable death toll they faced now. The result of this was that gun dealers were inundated with such prohibited weapons until they could be surrendered, or else deactivated to fall under the new guidelines.

One of these deactivation projects appeared in Enfield's hands on his last foray into the storeroom, and on a hunch, he flipped open the cardboard lid of a cartridge box and began to load the red plastic ammunition into the weapon he was holding. Expecting to be prevented from loading more than two, his eyes widened when he managed four and then slid open the breech to seat a fifth ready to fire.

He handed it to Johnson without a word, leaving him to marvel at the Remington pump action in his hands. It had no stock, instead ending in a pistol grip which sprouted a short loop of canvas strap to be slipped over his torso.

"Close encounters," Buffs said quietly, unwittingly echoing the words of their estranged SAS counterparts.

They carried everything back to their van, not bothering to take anything new except the shotgun which hung from the sergeant major, and they filed onwards to clear out the small convenience shop of everything they could find.

Clearing it for danger, of which there was luckily none, they filled plastic carrier bags with the remaining tinned food, as the smell inside the shop told them all they needed to know about the fresh produce. As they walked quietly and alertly back to the van, the noise of an engine widened their eyes.

Sounds from further into the town echoed along the eerily quiet channels between the buildings before another sound chattered into booming life; that of heavy gunfire.

"The others! The rest of your lot," Buffs said excitedly, seeing only dark looks on the faces of Johnson and Enfield.

"No," the bigger man said as his attuned ears recognised the difference in an instant, "that's thirty-cal."

Bufford looked at him uncomprehendingly until he explained.

"Ours only had gympies. Seven-six-two. That's not ours."

Bufford thought for a second before providing another explanation.

"What if they got one on resupply at the base?" he offered.

"What if they didn't?" Astrid countered, prompting the four of them to regard each other with something bordering on uncomfortable fear and a desperate hope.

"I'll go and check, then," Johnson said, taking a step forward and instantly wincing as he put pressure on his strapped ankle.

"No, you won't," Enfield said, ridding himself of any additional weight that could slow him down, which included the SA80 rifle as he unslung the Accuracy International. Buffs drew and offered him the Browning Hi-Power sidearm from his holster. Enfield shook his head to refuse it, tapping two fingers instead on the bayonet sheathed on his webbing, then doing the same to the large scope on his rifle.

"I'm not planning on getting anywhere near them, just going for a look."

The gunfire continued in disciplined bursts before two pauses and two longer salvos signalled the end of the one-sided gun battle, finishing with a final rattle of a few shots. Half a minute later, as the last clattering sounds of gunfire still echoed through the town, Enfield returned via an alleyway between two shops at a dead run, recklessly flying towards them in an awkward run as he pumped one arm, with the other clamping the rifle to his back to stop it bouncing. Needing no further explanation, they all piled into the van to leave in as much of a hurry as the slippery road allowed.

SIX

Nevin locked the hatch, pressing his face up to the viewport in time to see that the doorway was already piled up with the twice dead bodies which possessed the smell he still had in his nostrils. A kick to his shoulder between the bursts brought him back to his senses, making him put the headset back on in time to hear the voice of Michaels sounding every inch the Troop Sergeant he remembered.

"…cking brain in gear, you dozy wanker!" the voice said through the headset.

"What?" he answered.

"I *said*," Michaels growled as though the annoyance of repeating himself promised more peril to his driver than the dead outside their armoured ride, "push forward ten yards."

Nevin didn't respond, but he did as he was told and rolled the Ferret ahead in a straight line as instructed. The fire above him intensified as the bursts became longer. Michaels had rapidly filled the double doorway with dead and needed a change of angle so he could fire directly inside to hit the remaining zombies without wasting bullets by firing into the massed pile of meat. This continued for another eight or nine seconds until the firing stopped. A pause of the same time and another long burst opened up, making Nevin think that signalled the end of the engagement, before a final ripping period of sustained fire tore out.

"Go and check," Michaels said bluntly.

"Check fucking *what*?" Nevin snapped back, his voice an octave higher than normal.

"Check that there aren't any more coming out. See if I've just blocked the door or if they're all dead. I can't see all the way inside."

Nevin swallowed, his devious mind already imagining a life without someone telling him what to do, but he popped the hatch and took his submachine gun to climb down carefully and walk towards the building, without once taking his eyes off the pile of dead at the doors.

He stepped as close as he dared, seeing no movement and hearing no tell-tale sounds of any of them still mobile. He ran back to the Ferret, climbing up and closing down to lock the hatch again as he sat and shuddered.

"Well?" Michaels asked in a voice no longer edged with scorn.

"All dead."

"Good, drive on to the other end of the High Street. We'll wait for the others, then strip this place cle…"

"Ahead, movement," Nevin barked, cutting Michaels off. Both men looked ahead, seeing a flash of movement beside a building as a shadow ducked out of sight. While the person was no longer there, both men were left with a snapshot image of a shape pointing something in their direction. The something in question was undoubtedly a long rifle, and both men knew that the dead retreated when spotted about as often as they used weapons. The turret moved, and flame spat from the end of the barrel to erupt dust and chunks of brick from the corner of the wall where the person had disappeared. Michaels was no fool, and instead of firing at where the shape had been, he stitched a burst into the wall, knowing that they would over-penetrate and come out into the blind spot where the runner would likely be.

Nevin drove forwards to stop level with the alleyway as the turret rotated again to point directly down it. Nothing. Sure enough, the last rounds Michaels had fired had torn chunks through the soft obstacle of the brick, but no body lay on the ground.

"Who the fuck was that?" he asked Nevin.

"No idea, but the bugger was alive. And armed."

"Sod it, carry on," Michaels told him.

Nevin did as instructed again, the last incident all but forgotten but with a question rolling around in his head. He reformed the question before he asked it.

"They were shut in," he voiced, "Why bother?"

"Why bother wasting the ammo?"

"Well, yeah…"

"Nevin," Michaels said in a wistful tone, as though he was imparting some sage nugget of advice, "never leave an enemy in your rear. Ever."

———

"It was your man," Enfield said, breathless from his sprint and raising his voice for the others to hear while he stared out of the rear window of the van. Johnson was driving as fast as he could safely, keeping the truck in low gears to prevent the wheels spinning while he tried to keep the revs low and reduce their chances of being detected.

"Who?" Astrid asked from her position beside him as the others rode in the front, "Whose man?"

"One of the tankies," he said, eyes still glued to the road behind them and brick dust adorning his helmeted head like snowflakes, "that one who got the bloke killed, pissing about when we were getting supplies for the defences on the island. The one nobody liked."

Johnson's heart dropped, rising back up as though it was riding the crest of a wave of hate.

"Exactly what happened?" he asked loudly and carefully.

"Armoured car. Little one, like a Ferret but with a mounted HMG," Enfield recounted, "It rolled in and took out a load of Screechers coming out of a building, then your chap got out to check. He wasn't in uniform. Must have seen me, because they fired through the building line to where I'd been watching from."

Johnson's mouth set into a tight line, the blood draining from his lips as he squeezed them tight and gripped the wheel hard to make his knuckles do the same.

"It probably *was* a Ferret," he said, "with a turret-mounted thirty-cal. Rare as rocking horse shit. But if he was getting back in it, who fired on you?" he asked, knowing from experience how desperately cramped and claustrophobic the interior of those vehicles was, and certain that the gun would have to be manned to be driven and fired at the same time.

"Fuck knows," Enfield said, leaving relative silence inside the van until it was broken by Johnson's savage outburst that seemed to rise from his belly, until it poured from his mouth like so much vomited hatred, and it grew louder with each word.

"Fucking Nevin. That bone-idle, useless, thieving little shit-bag, *fuck!*"

Silence returned as their driver's breath came in growls.

"Mate of yours?" Buffs asked in a light tone.

"Mate? Fucking *mate?*" Johnson snarled, clearly feeling that it was too soon for levity, "He shirked off at every opportunity, started a pub brawl with our own fucking side when all this was going on, got a decent soldier and a good man killed by fucking about instead of doing his job, left his post to go looting and now, fucking *now*, he looks like he's gone fucking rogue…"

"Definitely not a mate, then," Buffs said, as though Johnson had helpfully cleared up the matter.

Almost under her breath, Astrid asked a rhetorical question of Enfield.

"Why does he always use this bad word like it is a comma?"

Enfield ignored her, keeping his eyes glued to their retreat for any sign of pursuit.

"No," came the growled response from the driving seat, "definitely not a mate, and whatever that little prick is up to, you can guarantee it's not good."

———

"Whoever it was," Michaels said in a voice that was clearly pissed off but tinged with a kind of wary respect for the mysterious person he had tried to kill, "they've done a decent job here." He turned to address the nervous gaggle of followers who darted their eyes everywhere as though they expected some undead abomination to emerge from a side street at any moment. "Come on in," he called to them, seeing the collective flinch at his raised voice, "grab everything and load it up."

He wandered outside, seeing the flow of his small crowd of followers part around him like water repelled by compressed air, and Nevin followed as his self-appointed right hand.

"Your old lot?" he asked his newest recruit and fellow deserter.

"Could be," Nevin said, "but I doubt it. If it was them, I'd expect more. They'd have a lot of the troopers on it, not to mention the bloody bootnecks and the *Sass* blokes."

"Hmm," Michaels growled ambiguously, not making it clear whether he understood Nevin's points or whether he was just concerned at having elite soldiers knocking about near his patch.

"I reckon they lost nearly half of the fighting men when I got away," Nevin opined, "and they weren't supposed to be heading this way, but further inland towards the north west."

"Hmm," Michaels growled again, more thoughtfully this time as he turned away and scanned the ground for something he didn't seem to feel like sharing just yet. He walked slowly, his head sweeping back and forth as he crossed the road, with the smallest of glances to either side which, as unlikely as traffic was, still demonstrated how ingrained some behaviours were in most humans. Nevin followed at a wary, respectable distance until he saw the man stop and stoop to the pavement. Nevin followed, leaning over the crouching man to see the trampled remains of a children's treat in his hand. The colourful foil wrapper had merged into the soft chocolate interior and all of that moulded to form a crust over the plastic capsule inside as it set harder in the chill temperatures.

Wordlessly, Michaels stood and dropped the detritus as though dismissing the clue as irrelevant.

"It doesn't matter," he said as he turned and strode back to the gun store, "Half the people left won't survive this winter anyway."

He chivvied their efforts, doubling them almost by his presence alone as the unspoken fear of his displeasure radiated outwards. They made no effort to sort or select anything, merely took the entire contents that weren't nailed down too securely, before loading it all into a van to be sorted when safely back on their hilltop. He led the way personally into the large freezer store, gun up and eyes narrowed, dispatching two of the things which were mostly dormant in a darkened rear stock room, before pulling shut the open door leading to the loading bay, and ordering everything to be taken. The restaurant part of his new home, taken by the threat of force alone against the unprepared and unsuspecting occupants, had a large walk-in freezer which could cope with most of what they took. When the vans were full, he ordered the place locked up again for a return trip when their supplies ran low. He knew that there would be fresh supplies coming each month from the survivors he intimidated but relying on other people wasn't something that the former sergeant did any more.

SEVEN

"Chop, chop," Nevin crowed petulantly at the human chain of 'volunteers' who had been ordered out into the cold to unload and sort the scavenged food on their return. He, like Michaels, believed in a hierarchy which dictated that the fighting men such as himself did not need to undertake the lowly tasks of cooking and washing clothes, as the ungrateful people under their protection should earn their keep. He stopped at a girl, thirteen or fourteen years old maybe, and grabbed her slender wrist after she had struggled to pass on an armful of frozen potatoes. His grip was too strong for her to pull away, so she froze still, her body weight leaning away from him in protest as she was powerless to resist any other way.

"What have you done here?" he asked, looking at the bright red skin denoting the fresh scars on her wrists, "Tried the coward's way out, did we?"

The girl summoned all of her strength to pull her arm away as her eyes flashed with bright, wet hatred and embarrassment. Nevin saw her doing this, and just as she set her stance to wrench her hand free, he let go of her, laughing as she fell heavily onto her backside to writhe in pain at the impact of her unsuspecting arse-cheeks hitting cold concrete. She stared back at him with undisguised hatred, her breath coming rapidly and raggedly through her nose as her mouth was set into a tight grimace to keep the tears of anger at bay. She found her feet as a kindly woman stepped directly in front of her.

"Go and help Ellie stack the freezer," she said, before adding a whisper of *"now."*

The girl went, without a backwards glance at the woman who had diverted her rage, or at the bastard who had invoked it.

The woman, Pauline, the original occupant of the historical site which had been preserved only through investment to turn it into a hotel and restaurant, went back to her task without saying anything to him, even though she desperately wanted to let her thoughts spew out in a torrent of indignant rage. She had taken the girl under her wing, much as she had with the older woman she had sent her to help after the bastards had dragged her away from her daughter to leave the little girl to a gruesome fate. That young woman, Ellie, had been deposited with Pauline, and she had looked after her as well as she could, even though the loss of her daughter left a gaping, ragged hole in her heart, which wasn't soothed at all by the tears she shed every night as she lay in bed thinking about what had happened to her.

Eventually the exhaustion of the thoughts combined with her tortured insomnia to render her into a state of unconsciousness more than sleep, and each morning she woke, having had a few precious moments more rest, she became able to function a little more every day.

She had resigned herself to her brutal and tragic loss now, seeking a reason to go on living after the certain knowledge of losing her baby girl had finally sunk in, and just when she was considering walking off the cliff, one of the raiding parties, as she thought of them, returned with fresh recruits to their community.

———

When Jessica had first been dragged away in the ambulance from her unhappy home life, she had fought hard against her lawful abductors. She tried to refuse the tablets they gave her, saying that she felt fine and didn't want to have anything to help her relax. The two nurses in white uniforms had held her down then, forcing open her mouth with something like a wooden spoon, and dropped two blue pills into her mouth. They tasted bitter, and she fought hard to spit them out, but her mouth was held closed, until her body betrayed her, and the natural swallowing reflex happened. The two still held her down as the ambulance leaned away from the bends in the road, for what seemed like mile after mile, until her arms and legs lost the power to push against them. It felt as if her whole body was numb, inside a bubble where the sounds and sensations of the outside world were muted and slowed somehow. She tried to speak, to curse them and demand to be let go, so that she could walk back and protect her little brother from the hell he had been left in. She couldn't speak. It was as if her lower jaw had been paralysed, and she was just drooling past her numb tongue when she tried.

Hours went by in that state when, unknown to her, it had been far less. The slowed passage of time in her drug-induced condition messed with her perception, giving her a sense of days passing with each minute. She was wheeled out of the ambulance after it stopped, reversing to bump the rear wheels against an unseen kerb. Somehow, she knew this; could picture it as though experiencing the end of the journey from an outside perspective. She fell further into that thought, allowing her mind to distance itself from her body as the wheels of the metal trolley she was strapped to clattered and bounced down the ramp and into the cooler dark interior through double doors. Strip lights flashed above her intermittently as she was transported deeper inside the white-walled interior, until she was left alone on the trolley directly under one of the lights, and she could hear voices that sounded muffled coming from a nearby room. One light, the one on the right to her perspective, flickered almost imperceptibly as though it kept phasing in and out so fast that nobody could see it. She could. She could see it clearly and even began to be able to predict when it would happen at irregular intervals. It blinked out for a long second, flickering back to life and radiating its yellowy glow outwards before anyone but her noticed. She began to think it was talking to her; like it was trying to communicate in some way to only her, as if they were both prisoners in this place, and neither could speak freely for fear of the nurses over-hearing them and foiling any plans they might make together.

I know, she told it in her mind, *we need to get out of here.*

———

She had been moved, had her clothes taken off her, and her wounded wrists dressed again with fresh bandages. She'd felt a sensation in those cuts when they were roughly wiped clean, and her brain told her that it registered that sensation as a stinging feeling, but somehow the connections to the part of her brain that felt pain were severed or blocked.

She had been dressed in a simple gown which was left open at the back when she was transferred onto a bed in a plain room, where every fixture was immovable and built into the walls. Eventually she managed to sit up, still feeling as though she was inside that same bubble, but as if the walls were growing thinner, allowing more of the terrible outside world to penetrate and send her confusing messages. Her mouth was dry, a sudden return of a normal feeling to her, and as though the room knew what she needed, her eyes found a plastic jug half-filled with water and a paper cup beside it. She poured herself some, getting nearly half of what she spilled over the lip of the jug into the cup, and drained it.

It seemed to her as if the water wasn't water at all, even though it tasted just like water, but was instead some elixir which woke her up and returned her full array of senses to her. With that return, after her fourth cup was raised to her mouth by her shaking hands, her memory returned with all the rage and hate and terror that she had missed out on when she had been in the bubble. She stopped drinking, turned her head slowly towards the thick off-white interior of the door without a handle, and threw the plastic jug at it with a high-pitched scream of rage.

The jug clattered off the door to clatter noisily on the floor in three bounces before it came to a spinning stop. As that sound disappeared, it was replaced by another, building in volume as it became multiple pairs of shoes moving with ominous purpose towards her door.

The shutter snapped open, revealing a pair of eyes on the other side of the thick Perspex viewing port, then it snapped closed again. She heard a chuckle from the corridor, followed by the sound of the shoes squeaking away in diminishing volume, until she was left alone with only the sound of her breath coming fast.

She ran at the door, bouncing off it as she screamed in rage and frustration, tears streaming down her face from the anger she was feeling, more than from any shred of weakness. The sounds of shoes returned with more purpose, menacingly stamping and squeaking along the corridor until the view port again revealed eyes, only this time narrowed in anger instead of wide with amusement. The shutter snapped across again, and a heavy clunk of a disengaging door lock echoed dully inside her empty cell.

The door spilled inwards, three grown men filling the gap in an instant as she was snatched up and off her feet to be piled back down onto the bed. She fought and screamed as they forced her wrists and ankles into the leather restraints, arching her back as she tried to bite them and use the only weapon available to her that they hadn't taken away.

They stepped back, out of breath and chuckling at the defenceless girl who was half the size of any one of them, so no match at all for all three. They left her alone, now unable even to reach her face to remove the sweat-sticky strands of hair out of her eyes. She stuck out her lower jaw and blew upwards, attempting to dislodge the annoyance that way, but gave up after a handful of attempts and lay back in angry exhaustion.

She had no idea how long she had been there, but the light from the single, high window grew dull. After her breathing had returned to normal, she felt cold, shivering as the cool air dried the sweat from her body and seemed to leave her permanently deprived of the body heat she had lost.

She lay there into the night, her cell lit only by the wan shaft of dull yellow from an external light outside the window, and she must have drifted in and out of consciousness because she had wet herself at some point. She'd heard footsteps a few times. Had heard the shutter squeak quietly open, as though whoever was peering in wanted to keep the animal in the cage undisturbed as much as possible, and in the depths of the night she heard another sound from the corridor which chilled her more than the low temperature could ever have done.

———

The outbreak had spread quickly from the separate section of the hospital, as the main building had been one of the epicentres of the local infection. Being a rural area, naturally the distance between hospitals capable of providing trauma care was often vast. Those attacked and bitten ahead of the main waves of dead flowing outwards from London were rushed to hospital, and in such confined areas where the sick and injured languished in beds, it made the rapid spread a forgone conclusion as the first of many critically ill patients died and then rose in a new form, in which their milky blind eyes zeroed in on the nearest victims.

One of the nurses from the Accident and Emergency department had been smoking outside a fire escape door when the screams and shouts of alarm first came from inside. She dropped her cigarette, grinding it out with her shoe by automatic reflex, looked inside and saw the man who had been brought in with the animal bite to his arm stomping almost drunkenly across the corridor with both arms raised towards an unseen target.

That makes sense, she thought, *drunk most probably. The bloke's burning a fever and blathering on about it being a man who's bitten him, when there's no way that's been caused by a person.*

Then the blood fountained past her view, making her hesitate and take an automatic step backwards away from the inexplicable horror she could see inside. The blood was followed by the drunken man on his hands and knees, snuffling at the hot, sticky liquid on the shiny floor. He froze, his head snapping up to lock his gaze directly onto her face as he sniffed the air with exaggerated animal-like movements.

She saw the eyes; milky and clouded as though he had been blinded by cataracts. The head tilted slowly to one side as the muscles of his body tensed before he flew at her.

He's not drunk, she decided, *that's not natural. Nobody should move like that.*

She stood transfixed by his approach as he slipped and slid

on the spilled blood, until her senses regained control of her terrified body and she reached out to slam the heavy door hard into his face. The door bounced back, revealing a writhing body crumpled in the doorway where the thick wood had impacted and rearranged his facial features hideously. He climbed back to his feet as she stood dumbstruck at what she was seeing and hearing from inside, and then she ran.

She ran faster than she had ever run before and wouldn't have thought herself capable of such a feat. She was not a small woman, nor would she ever class herself as athletic by any stretch of the imagination, but she propelled herself with an inhuman speed blindly across the road towards the nearest building set on higher ground.

Snuffling and grunting came from behind her until a hideous, terrifying noise ripped the air as though a set of bagpipes was being tortured on an inward breath. The guttural, primal scream the man emitted spurred her faster until she dared risk a glance behind her to see the man stumbling stiff-limbed closer to her.

The ambulance came from nowhere. Later she realised that her terror and focus had been so consumed by her attacker, by the predator hunting her down, that her brain must have filtered out the sound of the approaching engine and the screech of locked tyres and the sirens. It hit the man square, thumping him bodily through the air with a vile crunch of metal and bone to send him twenty paces down the road away from her. She froze again, unaware of how much her chest was heaving with the rapid breathing, and her instincts took over to send her two steps towards the sight of the injured man, despite the unnaturally violent behaviour he had exhibited. When she saw his broken and shattered limbs begin to move, saw him start to right himself with his ruined body and swivel his crooked neck back around to face her, all sense of helping the man vanished as quickly as it had first appeared, all duty of care evaporated in a heartbeat, and she turned and ran again as other afflicted men and women spilled from the main building.

Going via the rear entrance to the other building, if only to seek sanctuary inside away from the monsters she feared were chasing her, she ran inside and turned to bolt the doors behind her. She ran through the corridors, finding some doors locked and others open to her.

Too late, she found the suddenly familiar sounds of screams and screeches from ahead, and faltered, turning back to bump chest first into a white-uniformed orderly running towards the sounds.

"No," she pleaded, "don't go that way."

"I've got to…" he started to say before she slapped him to focus his attention.

"No! You've got to get us out of here. Right now. People have gone mad," she told him, "they're… *killing* each other."

He hesitated for a second, seeing nothing but the maniacally desperate look in her eyes, then led her away from the terrible sounds. He hesitated again, his hands fluttering at the keys clipped on his waist as he slowed and turned to her.

"I've got to help them," he said as he thrust the keys at her, "get as many people out as you can, just don't open any of the doors with a red card by them."

She swallowed, nodded, and watched the man jog away as his shoes squeaked on the floor. Left in silence, she turned and walked to the nearest door to peer through the thick glass of the observation window. She glanced away, checking the details of the name and the colour-coded card beside the door. She saw that it bore a piece of red card underneath the legend of a name, surname first, and she looked back inside just as something hit the glass with a wet thud.

She recoiled, stepping back as the fresh shit smeared slowly down with gravity and the cackling laugh bounced around the concrete walls within.

That one can stay there, she told herself, moving down the corridor until she found a door without a coloured card. She looked through, her breath catching as she saw a young girl strapped to the bed looking small and helpless in the leather restraints. She paused, glancing hesitantly at the lack of colour-coordinated risk assessment, and she made a judgement call in the desperate hope that she was right. Fumbling with the keys, she unlocked the door.

———

Jessica thought back to that day often. Now, as she hauled frozen bags of potatoes and vegetables onto shelves in the huge freezer, she wondered where her younger brother was, and if he had survived, too.

EIGHT

ECHO-ONE-ONE, CHARLIE-ONE-ONE. SITREP: NO LOSSES TO C-1-1. CONSOLIDATED POSITION AT 50.8734N, 2.8915W WITH MIXED CIVILIAN AND OTHER ARMS PERSONNEL. SUPPLIES LOW BUT SUSTAINABLE AT PRESENT. SURVIVORS IN EXCESS OF 100 REQUIRE EXTRACTION. CONFIRM VIABILITY OF SECURE LOCATION.

The message on the small screen was short and to the point, and it also had to be sent when the four-man SAS team were safely away from prying eyes at the big house. Privacy was not something many people could enjoy on any military base, and Major Downes had yet to bring Captain Palmer up to speed on the other deployments of special forces troops. That would have been so far beyond his original pay grade that his need to know had gone from night to day.

"Keep it on, Smiffy," he said, meaning for his trooper to preserve the integrity of the complex snaking antenna cables used to send the burst data transmission on one of the set frequencies programmed into their man-portable radio, "we'll give them an hour and pack it up."

"No need, Boss," Smiffy said, "getting one back now."

Downes damn near bowled the man out of the way as he pushed his face up to the small readout to take in the answering message.

CHARLIE-ONE-ONE, ECHO-ONE-ONE. NO LOSSES TO ECHO TEAMS. OUR LOCATION IS VIABLE AND DEFENDED. SUPPLIES ADEQUATE. UNABLE TO SEND EVAC BY AIR. RECOMMEND JOURNEY BY VEHICLE OR BOAT VIA SHALLOW COASTAL WATERS ONLY. REPEAT, VEHICLE OR SHALLOW COASTAL WATERS ONLY.

"Well, bugger me…" Downes said to himself.

"Rather not, Boss," Mac intoned from behind him, "I'm more of the blonde hair, big boobs and daddy issues type." Downes ignored the levity and explained.

"Major Kelly has four bricks under his command," he said, using the slang term for the four-man teams they usually operated in at the coalface level, "and they were in London as soon as that lab went dark. They were sent for a selection of VIPs and evac'ed by helicopter to a place designated 'Echo'."

The three other men of his tightly-bound team exchanged looks. Only Mac's face remained impassive, as the other two were learning about this for the first time.

"We've still got a government?" Dez asked.

"Of a sort," Downes answered, "but I rather suspect they're being kept safe for whatever comes after. They are set up for this, the quarantine I mean, and something tells me they aren't scratching around for flour and yeast like we are."

Smiffy read over the response again, asking why the need to emphasise the shallow water approach.

"Because whatever is left of NATO's naval forces will probably sink anything seen leaving the British or Irish mainland, I imagine," Downes answered. "Send an acknowledgement," he instructed his trooper.

Smiffy pressed the buttons on the backpack-sized device attached to the lengths of wires, then began collapsing the equipment and packing it back down to be stowed in the rear of their Land Cruiser taken for the reconnaissance mission at the request of Palmer.

"You wait," Smiffy said as he hauled the ungainly radio up and into the tailgate, "one day we'll be able to do this from our personal mobile telephones."

"Dream on, laddy," Mac drawled, "you just focus on the job we're doing before you get all that Star Trek nonsense in your head. What are you after? A phone call from your watch?"

Smiffy shrugged. His job was to get the job done, whatever it might be. Unlike the rest of the army, where a man or woman would have one main job and maybe learn how to undertake the roles of the others around them until their experience grew sufficiently that they understood the bigger picture, he had lots of jobs. He was a sniper and a signalman, being well-versed in long-range communications as well as long-range killing. He was part engineer, part infantryman, part paratrooper, as well as being a half-decent medic, as they all were. That was what marked them out as different; not their size or natural ability, but their attitude and their resource for learning.

"So, what's the deal with this secure site, Boss?" Dezzy asked gently, not wanting to get shut down for raising the subject. Downes stopped folding the map he had been looking at back to its original dimensions, pausing as though he was giving serious thought as to whether he should share the information in full. He resumed his folding with a sharp intake of breath, as though the moment of introspection had robbed him of the ability to inhale, and he stuffed the map into his bag.

"Scotland. Inner Hebrides to be more exact," he explained, "isolated and well stocked, and hopefully they should be able to see out the infection, or whatever it is, and return to re-establish order. I thought it was a badly kept secret, but obviously not. They've been planning this as a fall-back space for years in case of bio or nuclear attack; they've built bunkers and stockpiled God knows what. There can't be too many of us left, probably even fewer after this bloody winter ends, and there will be a lot of rebuilding to do."

"How does that affect us?" Smiffy asked as he leaned on the side of the truck.

"How do you think?" Mac butted in and answered for the Major, "Every house, every shop, every factory and every farm in the whole bloody UK needs clearing." His words left them all quiet as the prospect of surviving brought with it even more challenges.

"I mean, come on," Mac went on, "we've seen how they freeze up in this weather, and my guess is that they'll degrade somehow when the weather warms again, but that doesn't stop the faster ones much now, does it?"

Nobody answered his rhetorical question.

"Mac's right," Downes said, "we know they go into a kind of hibernation, and any that have followed any Limas inside buildings and gone into winter mode will still be dangerous when they," he waved his hand vaguely to try and demonstrate the word he was looking for in vain, "when they... *snap out of it* or whatever. Fuck me, lads, even *one* of them left could end the world all over again. That's how it started this time."

Dezzy looked at him, taking in his words and not wanting to lose any more time, or focus on the future of what ifs. He glanced at Smiffy, the two men feeling ever responsible for one another, and both shot the other a look that said it didn't matter much to them anyway. They'd just do their jobs.

An hour passed, which had been spent in near silence as they systematically cleared a small village door-to-door, just as they had discussed doing all over their afflicted country in order to get life back to normal. Towards the end of the main road which passed as the High Street, their tactics evolved, as there could be only a few of the enemy remaining in the village, even if they were alerted to their presence, and the team began to make more noise.

The far end of that stretch, nothing more than a reduced speed limit on a section of winding road, held a huddle of houses set back on one side before the road opened up into countryside views again.

"Smiffy," Downes said in a low voice, "push up to the GLF and hold. Dezzy, on me, ready for the door. Mac, take tail."

None of them answered, but all dropped into their allocated positions. Dez would open the door, one way or another, and Downes would enter with Mac behind him, while Smiffy kept an eye on the road in both directions from the iconic road sign which had put a smile on the face of any person who had undertaken a fast driving course. The white circle with a diagonal black flash, denoting a derestricted speed limit or, as they liked to call it, *Go Like Fuck.*

Dez put a hand on the doorknob, pausing to glance at the other two men and receiving a nod to continue, and then he turned the handle to find it locked. That in itself was rare in those parts, but you'd never expend the energy of kicking down a door unless you had to. The air of tension ebbed noticeably as the three men knew they had a longer respite before action was required, and Mac moved to press his face to a downstairs window and check for movement.

Dezzy lowered his weapon on its sling, placing both gloved hands on the cold wood of the door and pressing to see where it flexed and where it was solidly secured. It bent inwards at the bottom on the same side as the lock, but the topmost corner on that side was annoyingly rigid.

"Bolted," Dez said softly. He didn't need to explain that this meant it was locked securely from the inside. "Go around?"

"Takes us past the other houses we haven't cleared," Downes said, "We go in this way."

Dez nodded, holding out a hand to gesture his Major back away from the door as he reached behind himself to free the automatic shotgun. He raised the gun to his shoulder, checked behind him to see that the others weren't too near to him, turned his face away and fired.

Mac hadn't seen any movement inside, because the window he had peered through looked straight in at a wall. Had they moved further around the outside of the house and explored further, then they would have found the family of five still securely locked inside their home. They might have been secure, but they certainly weren't safe.

The mother, complete with apron sheeted in blood where she had chewed on the hands, faces and necks of her own children, turned and cocked her head quizzically at the small creaks coming from her front door. It bent inwards slightly, flexing in the bottom corner before her ears detected something that made no cognitive connection, but instead translated into a primal feeling that there was prey nearby.

She turned to face it fully, feet shuffling on the spot before her stiff and seized legs took tentative steps towards it. The door was beautifully crafted, carved from a single piece of oak many years before any of them had been born, and it had hardened with age to be like stone. She heard clicks, voices, and the shuffle of a boot on stone, but again none of these sounds connected to any memories or made any associations in her brain, despite which she was spurred onwards regardless. Behind her, disturbed by her movement and suddenly reanimated state, her children followed in reverse order of height with her eldest child looking over the heads of what had been his two younger sisters before their once-loving mother had changed them into what they now were.

Finally finding her voice, the mother contracted the muscles in her chest to draw in a breath and with it the start of the dry-throated, creaking, shrieking noise they'd made when they'd heard noises outside their home. Since then, since that giant herd of people like they were, had passed through to leave them behind in silence and solitude, they hadn't been stimulated enough to make that noise. But now, as their once-mother reached out a bony and emaciated hand towards the front door, her mouth let it out to tear the stale air in their home.

With a shattering *BOOM,* the top quarter of the door disintegrated, letting in a rush of cold, fresh air, as if their house had been a sealed ship in the vacuum of space. The splinters of wood from the sudden opening fanned out, some striking the woman and embedding themselves into her skull and face, but one flew straight and true into her open mouth to puncture the soft wall at the back and drive the wicked spike of hard wood through the sinew and flesh. It punctured her spinal column high up and cut off the unthinking synapses which powered her arms and legs, and made her slump into a heap, effectively blocking her children from reaching the front door before it burst the rest of the way open to silhouette a big man in the aperture.

As one, they all shrieked in attack.

———

Dezzy fired a single shot into the wood where he thought the troublesome bolt was, shattering the door and creating a noise, ruinous and huge in the silent confines of the small village. He followed it up with the ballistic application of boot sole to the door just beside the lock. Utterly satisfied with both the mechanical and personal destruction he had just wrought, he stood in the doorway to assess his work. And swore ever so briefly but loudly.

He didn't think, not like the way that the Screechers didn't think, but more of a naturally human instinctive reaction. He just raised the gun already in his hands and triggered off five shots into the horrifying abominations reaching for him. He stood frozen, looking over the barrel of the demonic close-quarters tool, disgusted and horrified at what he had just done, until he was shoved aside bodily to crunch into the splintered doorframe. Before Dezzy could right himself and bring his weapon back up to face the threat which had caused the man behind him to act, he heard a pair of muted cracks in rapid succession followed by the sound of a lifeless body slumping to the floor.

Downes hauled his demolition expert back up to his full height, releasing him before stepping into the room with his MP5 held in tight to his shoulder and swinging it left and right to cover the room. Mac bustled in beside him, mirroring his movements to provide maximum speed as they cleared the dank smelling interior of the house. Dez stayed where he was in the doorway, almost panting and unable to control his breathing as he stared down at the horror and gore he had created in a second of unexpected and brutal violence.

A hand clamped onto his shoulder, making him jump and turn on the attacker as he raised the butt of his shotgun, intending to connect it to the skull of whatever had crept up on him when he had dropped the ball of concentration. The blow was blocked, and his eyes met the icy-blue reflection of Smiffy's.

"It's me, Dez," he told him, "it's me."

Dezzy slumped, a half gasp of a stifled sob escaping his mouth, which made his friend lean over his shoulder at the destruction inside. Smiffy's eyes went dull, glazing over as he saw, assessed, understood, dealt with and moved on; all in an instant.

"You had no choice," he said to his friend, lightly slapping his face to bring their eyes back together, "Hey? You hear me? You had no choice. It's shit, but it's done. Now get yourself together."

He held him by the shoulders for a few seconds, letting Dez' exaggerated breathing stabilise and watching as the oxygen and good sense returned him to his former self. Dez stood tall, emotionally dusting himself off, and walked inside to step over the three headless bodies of the young children as they lay collapsed in a meat pile in between their twice-dead parents.

NINE

"Major," Lloyd greeted the leader of the SAS team as he slid out of the passenger side of the truck. Downes walked to the leader of the marines and shook his hand.

"Lloyd," he answered, scanning his eyes over the twenty men and two big transport trucks arrayed behind him at the agreed meeting place.

"All quiet down there?" the younger man asked, indicating the village in the shallow ground ahead.

Downes hesitated, recalling the initial look on the face of his man, usually so stalwart, reliable and unflappable, when he had first cleared that last house below and ahead of them.

"It is now," he answered enigmatically, "Want us to hang around?"

"Could you?"

Before answering, Downes looked first at his watch and then up at the sky, which was grey and held an air of veiled malevolence.

"May as well," he said, "we aren't going to get another village cleared before sundown and before this weather closes in."

Lloyd had to agree, having had the luxury of time to make his own guesses about the newest weather front as they waited for their scouts to return.

"I'll put two at each end of the village," Downes said, "If you hear us shooting, then pack up and get ready to move."

"Understood," Lloyd answered, turning to his men and shouting for them to load up, and instructing them that her Majesty wasn't paying them to stand around and look pretty.

"They ain't paying us at all, Sir," came a disembodied voice from somewhere near a tail ramp.

"Enough of your treasonous comments, Foster," Lloyd snapped half in jest, recognising the voice instantly despite the speaker's obvious attempts to hide his identity, "but well done on volunteering to be the first man in. Proud of you, lad."

Milton, three years the Lieutenant's senior, smiled in the back of one of the trucks. He had no qualms about being the first man in, especially seeing as the Hereford lot had just been through, which minimised his chances of getting eaten. He had made the joke in the clear knowledge that the officer would return fire with some admonishment and raise the morale of the boys in the process.

He had been offered promotion, told, even, that he would be wearing three chevrons on his sleeve, but he had been adamant that he didn't want it. After being summoned by Lieutenant Lloyd to the office where Captain Palmer ran things, he had stood to attention and kept his eyes resolutely forward until told to stand easy.

"Relax, man," Palmer had said smoothly. Lloyd explained to Foster why he wanted him to take the rank, detailing the primary reasons that he was liked and respected by the surviving marines.

"You fought well on the island," Lloyd said, "and the boys listen to you."

"Then I'll keep doing that, Sir," Foster answered, "but I don't want the stripes."

"Why is that?" Palmer had asked, genuinely intrigued as to why a man would turn down such an honour. Foster smiled.

"It's not like there's a pay bump, Sir," he said, pushing the luck of his flippancy as far as he dared, "and if I'm a sergeant, I have to enforce the rules and make the lads scared of me. I can't have a laugh to lift their spirits if I'm doing that."

Lloyd thought about their last sergeant, the irritable, irascible and ever-grumpy Bill Hampton. He was like a father to the marines, always looking after them and making sure that they all had the right kit and that none of them went without, but that fatherly attitude harked back to a time when the whip was still an acceptably used tool for facilitating learning. He could be harsh, very harsh on the men if they let him down, and that was the aspect of the role that Foster was trying to refuse to undertake.

"Thank you, marine, you may go now," Lloyd had said to him, returning the parade ground crisp salute, which he felt was for Palmer's benefit, a display to maintain the high standards and expectations of his corps.

"I rather suspect, Christopher," Palmer drawled, "that the man has a point. My advice, if you need any at all, which I highly doubt is the case, is to encourage him to promote the morale of the men without forcing the rank on him."

Palmer looked up, checking to see whether his conversational advice was being taken as such and not interpreted as an order.

"Your unit is, sadly, smaller now and the men look directly to you for leadership. I say keep him close and mentor the man; bring him into command discussions and see how he thinks."

"You're probably right, Julian," Lloyd answered, knowing

that the shrewd-minded young man was indeed entirely accurate.

In the front of the truck, Lloyd also smiled as he finally understood Foster's point. He could not have reproved his sergeant that way, nor could he expect to tolerate the quips that the man made which required the reprimands he found himself giving out. But the balance was perfect. Foster worked hard and played hard, the men looked to him for their lead and despite his humorous comments, the unit was cohesive.

As the trucks set off down the gentle slope in the undulating land, Lloyd tucked his cold chin into the scarf around his neck and kept his eyes resolutely ahead on their target.

———

It took a little over three hours for the small village to be cleared, which was far faster than they had been when they'd first trialled their new tactics. The plan was simple; SAS team go in and do reconnaissance, clear out any small elements of hostile forces, then withdraw. After that, the main body of troops would move in, seal off the village and systematically empty each building of everything useful to be brought back to the large estate they occupied. Anything too large for the trucks would be safely stockpiled and returned for, and any return trip would be conducted with strong numbers because, as they had learned all too often, the situation could change from shit to deadly in an instant when dealing with an unthinking and unpredictable enemy.

Downes had sent his driver, Smiffy, to the furthest end of the village in the truck with Mac so that he could keep Dezzy close to him and wait for the man to speak about what had phased him so badly. He didn't push him as they sat on a low roof in the cold air covering the closest end of the village's approach road, but simply waited for him to speak.

Dez sat still and quiet, wanting to strip and clean the shotgun for no other reason than to purge the barely-coked barrel of the weapon of the evidence that he had fired it, as though somehow that would clean away the memory of what he had done. He had done the right thing, but he was a mature enough and experienced enough soldier to know that a person didn't know what would affect them until it had already affected them. He was tough, he was switched-on, but he also knew that he had been affected by the suddenness of the attack. He knew that he had been affected by his instant, and correct, reaction to open fire.

He considered the other ways it could have played out.

He could have baulked, not taken the shot, and he could have been infected. Downes could have been infected. Mac. Smiffy.

In a world where 'us or them' held even fewer moral obligations than before, what he had done made perfect sense, both morally and tactically, but he had still pulled the trigger and violently decapitated three young kids with a brutal and evil storm of lead. He knew they weren't children, not really, not anymore, but he would forever be left with the images of their small skulls breaking apart under his onslaught.

"You okay?" Downes asked softly, wanting to move things on more quickly than they were occurring naturally. Dez took a breath, held it, and blew it out with puffed cheeks before responding.

"Yeah, Boss," he said as he strapped the shotgun back onto his pack, "I'm fine."

"Good lad," Downes said quietly, his eyes narrowing as he diverted some of his attention away from the stilted conversation and towards the distant countryside. Dez saw his look, followed his eyeline and scrabbled with a belt pouch to retrieve the small binoculars which he raised to his eyes and asked, "Where?"

"My eleven o'clock," Downes said, not having to explain to the seasoned soldier beside him that he had detected movement, "Stone wall, west towards the higher ground. Gateway."

Dez followed the instructions he had been issued with as effectively as possible in such few words. They had become expert at this, so in tune with one another after the months they had spent in Afghanistan, where they were more likely than not to be fired upon by the side they were unofficially there to help than by any Soviet conscripts. Then, just as now, only in a very different way, failure to detect the enemy's movement could easily result in death.

"Got it," Dez said, his face contorted as he squinted into the eyepiece of the futuristic-looking binoculars, "Screecher. Can't seem to figure out the gate. Here."

Dez held out the binos to Downes, who took them wordlessly. It took him only a second to acquire the moving smudge on the horizon and magnify it into a filthy and ragged approximation of what it had once been.

Most of the right arm from just below the elbow was missing, and the right side of what seemed to have once been light blue denim dungarees was sheeted black with gore. The skin of the face, drawn back as though stretched by malnutrition from teeth which now seemed overly large, was far paler than even the other dead they had encountered. It moved sluggishly, drunkenly, as it bumped its small chest into the wooden bars of the gate, unable to comprehend why the way forward was closed to it. Downes watched closely, his own face screwed up just as Dezzy's had been, as the thing stopped trying to weakly force its way through the obstacle and instead turned its nose up to the sky and seemed to sniff the air, tasting it like an animal would. It threw back its head, mouth open to emit that awful screeching noise that so aptly lent them the nickname given by the soldiers; but no sound reached them.

Major Downes had fought many enemies of Her Majesty

over many years of conflict, but never, not even when low on ammunition and pinned down by superior forces, had he experienced a fear of an enemy as he did then. Unbelievably, impossibly, the thing seemed to slowly lower its head and cock it over to one side as it stared its sightless stare directly at Downes from nearly three hundred metres away. Despite himself, Downes shuddered.

"Smiffy could have it with his VAL," Dez said gently, suggesting that the stolen Russian sniper rifle be brought back, along with its operator, to dispatch the creature.

"It's too far off to cause us any bother," Downes said, feigning a relaxed manner that he did not fully believe himself, "Just keep an eye on it and hope it doesn't have friends around here."

"Friends?" Dez asked, the binoculars pressed to his eyes once again, "It can barely move, let alone organise a search party."

And it couldn't, Downes realised. It could barely walk. It couldn't climb a simple wooden five-bar gate that any five-year-old could scale with ease. It also looked, he thought hopefully, like it was starving to death.

"See anything?" a voice called out from below them, startling both men, who had the presence of mind and body not to let it show.

"Just one of them," Dez called down softly to the marines officer, "no bother to us."

———

They didn't make it back before the rain, but they did beat nightfall. Two very heavily loaded trucks grunted and chugged their way through the intricate defences cut into the ground now frozen solid and showing no signs of returning to the slippery mud it had been not long after creation. The grubby

Toyota truck behind them, its own engine barely even breathing hard in comparison, rolled in behind as the men on duty replaced the heavy barricades of wood and wire over the one stretch of approach not cut by the hastily dug moat.

Downes sent his men back to their small corner of the big house, not needing to remind any of them about keeping their mouths shut about the contact they had made with other clandestine troops, and he went to find Palmer. Ordinarily, he would have relinquished his MP5 for one of his men to clean it while he talked officer stuff, but the thought of anyone being further away than the length of their arm to their weapon was utterly abhorrent.

"Ah, Major! Pleasure to see you, do come in," Palmer exclaimed as soon as he entered the parlour-cum-office.

It wasn't the Palmer he was expecting, however. In place of the competent and charismatic Captain, he found the entitled and spoilt younger version. The apple who had evidently rolled after it had fallen from the family tree.

"Second Lieutenant," Major Downes coldly greeted the boy who was opening and closing cupboards and drawers with tuts of annoyance each time he came up empty. Downes guessed what the boy was after, and intentionally kept his hand still from wanting to reach for his back pocket and the small half-bottle of brandy tucked flat against his right buttock. It was rough stuff, clearly no expensive vintage and more of an access tool for a person to find that painless space where stresses and worries no longer affected them, but it didn't matter much; he had taken it on a whim after seeing that Palmer, *Captain* Palmer, had run out.

"I suspect," Lieutenant Palmer said theatrically in his nasal whine, "that you are after my older brother? Alas, he is not here, as you can see. Might I recommend you try the kitchens."

"The kitchens?" Downes responded before he could stop himself and simply walk off and ignore the privileged whelp.

"Yes," Palmer said with theatrical relish, "it seems he's decided to forgo any further career soldiering and become a *scullery maid.*" Palmer junior invested all the scorn and mockery he could manage, which was a very significant amount as it turned out, into his distaste for the serving classes. The Major, well-bred from a respected family in his own right, ignored the sullen lack of manners as Palmer refused to acknowledge the officer's superior rank. That kind of divide, that kind of overt disrespect, was likely to be a result of the combination of Palmer's inherent feelings of superiority through birth right, and the bizarre stress they all felt, which broke down the normal bounds of military discipline. Despite the beliefs of the enlisted men, the officer classes still obeyed a set of strict rules when in their own company.

Without another word, Downes turned on his heel and propelled his tired body towards the kitchens with long strides.

There he found that the younger brother was partly correct, as the older brother was indeed rubbing shoulders with the common folk. And he seemed to be having the time of his life doing so.

The raucous laughter of women filled the room that Downes had walked into, and the Captain looked up, wearing a somewhat sheepish expression as his bare forearms, the sleeves of his uniform shirt rolled up above the elbows, were dusted with flour. His expression darkened slightly, as though the weight of responsibility and his leadership had found him and threatened to drag him back to the present, and he stopped what he was doing.

Downes stared at him, and a smile crept over his face.

"I saw the women making their dough in Afghanistan," he began, "and I rather think they put their backs into the task a damned sight harder than you are, Captain."

Palmer smiled, laughing with the others at him being caught out. Instead of ruining his small moment of fun,

Downes instead rolled up his own sleeves and washed his hands in the deep porcelain sink set into the thick wood of the kitchen worktop. He shook them dry, accepting an offered towel from a woman nearby, and dried his hands as he looked down at his dirty clothing. The kitchen was warm, perpetually warm in fact, which is why he suspected that the women and children had a tendency to gather there. It was usually occupied in one form or another, day and night. He stripped off the black smock he was wearing, exposing layers of clothing underneath, and he smiled sweetly at the woman who had taken back the towel.

"May I?" Downes asked as politely as he could, indicating the white, frill-edged pinafore adorning her ample frame. The women laughed even more now, Palmer joining in with them thinking that it was a joke. It wasn't. Downes slipped the white top of the apron over his head and tied the waist straps with fast efficiency before joining Palmer at the worn butcher's block he was working at.

"Now the key, I'm told," Downes said as he took his own lump of dough and slapped it down onto the surface to dust it with flour, "is to work it hard and rapidly. Am I right, Mrs Maxwell?" he asked the woman beside Palmer.

"You're very right, Major," Denise Maxwell answered, "I never knew you secret-squirrel lot got taught the finer points of baking."

"Join the British army and see the world," Downes told her with a conspiratorial smile, "I think we both fell for that one, eh, Julian?"

"I do believe we did, Major," Palmer said as he began to use the heel of his right hand under the stiff arm to dig his weight into the dough.

"What have you got there, Major?" Denise asked, pointing at the protrusion from his back pocket.

"Ah, yes, I almost forgot," he said as he carefully retrieved the small bottle by the neck with forefinger and thumb, so as not to cover both himself and the bottle in flour, "Captain? I thought you might appreciate this."

Palmer looked at the bottle, pretending not to show his mild horror at both the paltry size and the unknown maker of the brandy on offer.

"You have my thanks indeed, Major," he said, "only I worry that the ladies will feel us to be somewhat misogynistic should we take a brandy in their domain, as such…"

"Oh, don't you worry about us," another woman chimed in, speaking slowly as she bumped her hip into Denise Maxwell's and reached into the back of a kitchen cupboard, "we manage just fine, thank you very much," she said as she produced a massive bottle of scotch and a handful of china mugs held expertly in her fingers.

They drank. They kneaded dough for the fresh bread they would enjoy the next morning, and in a frozen world of shit, they found a moment of happiness.

TEN

"We need to go outside. We need to go into the city for supplies."

Mike Xavier closed his eyes tightly and pinched the bridge of his nose. He had heard this from Jean-Pierre for the last week, after he had tried and failed to find another solution to their supply issue.

"For fuck's sake, JP," Xavier said, "we've been through this. Where can we go? What can we find? The city is full of them, they still wander up to the fence every day, we can't ju…"

"They have not come for more than a week," Jean-Pierre cut him off, "and when they do, they can barely walk. They are slow. We can make it."

"Can we?" Xavier answered, "and if we don't make it back, then who is looking after the others? They'll fall apart without leadership, and I know we never asked for it, but it's in our hands now. I say we stay here, sit tight and ride out the bad weather."

Jean-Pierre, tall and still heavily muscled despite the shortage of food, glowered at his captain on the very edge of insolence and disobedience, before he withdrew a step and shrunk away slightly as though he was endeavouring to power down the passionate anger he felt at the situation.

"I am sorry, Captain," he said in a softer voice, yet one still edged with steel, "but we cannot do this. There is not enough food to go around as it is. We need more, or people will try to leave themselves. You forget what happened yesterday?"

Captain Xavier had not forgotten. He remembered only too well having to fight his way to the head of the crowd to beat people back from what remained of their meagre food stores. They had consolidated everything weeks before, keeping a central reserve of supplies which were issued on an equal basis, and that had taken up four of his crewmen to guard it day and night. An angry mob had formed late in the day, borne of desperation instead of malice or greed, and the stores had been broken into. One of his men had been knocked out cold, his scalp pouring blood from where the lump of wood had cracked him hard over the skull without warning. Xavier had led the charge to restore order, far too much noise being made in the process, and by the time he had pushed back the desperate raiders and laid into them, shouting, he turned to see that most of the food had gone. He threw his body into one thief, one cowardly raider who tried to scurry past him with an armful of items, and his body weight checked them hard off their feet into the metal walls of the container to ring a low, dull bell sound as they slumped to the ground. The hood and scarf fell back to reveal the dirty, terrified face of a woman who was clutching fearfully the can of tinned pears in her hand. Xavier, ashamed of himself and embarrassed about the actions of the thieves, couldn't bring himself to punish the woman any further than he had and turned away from her.

JP wasn't there; he had been at the gates where he spent most of his time under a brooding cloud of ominous gloom. Had he been, Xavier reckoned that the men and women who'd attacked his crewmen out of desperation would have looked at the shadowy embodiment of terror and decided that they had somewhere else to be. But he wasn't there, and they were brave enough or scared enough to break into the food stores and destroy their last chance at stretching out what food they had left. He had restored order, forcibly detained the few people under his protection who had been caught stealing and spread the word fast and clear that he wanted anything taken to be returned, or else there would be consequences. He didn't know what those consequences would be, nor how he would enforce them, but none of the supplies were returned, regardless of the threat.

Now he faced a number of dilemmas. He had a decision to make about what to do with the people his crew members were currently guarding, and that decision would open another can of worms when those protesting at their incarceration didn't get their way. He had to decide how to ensure that his own men stayed loyal when one of them was badly hurt, because their dedication was wavering by being faced with such uncertainty. Most of all, he knew he had to find more food before the survivors tore each other to pieces.

"One problem at a time, JP," he said quietly, "one problem at a time."

"What do you mean, Captain?"

"I mean we can't ignore what happened yesterday, but we can't ignore *why* it happened either. We need food, but we need to deal with the discipline problem. If we were at sea, what would we do?"

"At sea? Then your word would be the law."

"Exactly, but we're not at sea. We're in port, and we're stuck here. If we set sail then we'll be sunk, and if we stay then we'll starve or rip each other apart. Which leaves us with what?"

"We go into the city," Jean-Pierre said as he banged a big fist onto the desk beside his captain, "and we bring back food.

We control the food and we control the people. We double the guard on the supplies."

"Is that who you want to be?" Xavier asked with genuine curiosity in his voice.

"Who I want to be?" Jean-Pierre shot back, "I want to be alive, and I want to take charge of these people because none of them, *none of them,* can keep the whole group safe, other than you and me."

Xavier stared at his right-hand man, his huge enforcer, and he shook his head slowly as a smile crept over his face.

"I hate to say it, JP," he said after a resigned sigh, "but you're right. For the greater good and all that. Okay, get everyone together and I'll talk to them."

———

The crowd assembled below Mike Xavier was a mixed spectrum of human emotion. The angriest of them were either at the front, venting their frustrations and indignation at him loudly, or else at the back keeping quiet. Those quiet ones were who scared him, as they were the ones most likely to try something stupid and get them all hurt or worse. The tired, broken, apathetic ones occupied the middle of the crowd as they just stared and listened in weary resignation to whatever fate would be decided for them by others. The scared and depressed faces looked up at him, interspersed occasionally with one or two faces showing a rictus of misplaced anger at him, and he held up his hands to wait for enough silence to descend on them for him to speak. Finally, hoping that the angry concentration of voices hadn't stirred up anything unwelcome and attracted the kind of attention they had spent months avoiding, he lowered his hands and spoke.

"We've been here too long to let it all fall apart now," he said, "we've survived too long to just give up and rip into each other over a tin of beans. What happened here yesterday *cannot happen ever again.*" He placed heavy emphasis on each individual word, and then he paused, scanning the faces, seeing that most of the hostility was still there but some of it had begun to transform into confused attention. He went on.

"I am to blame for this," he said, his hand held flat on his chest, "I am to blame because I allowed this to happen, but no more. No more. We need food," he said as he started to pace up and down the raised platform he was standing on to be seen as he spoke. "We need more food, but who's gonna risk their lives to find it?" he stared out at the small crowd, daring them to answer his rhetoric. When nobody spoke he carried on. "Do you expect me and my crew to risk our lives for you? Do you expect us to keep you safe? To feed you? To protect you and just roll over when you attack us? Do you?" he glowered at them, seeing that some of the angry faces had turned into downcast looks of shame. "Of course you don't, because the people who did this weren't thinking. But we are going to get past what happened, and we're going to start by sharing the risks."

He stopped talking, dropping down from his platform to walk through the assembled crowd and look into their faces as he spoke again.

"My crew and I will lead the way, but you all need to help. We'll go out there, we'll put our lives on the line, but you will too," he paused to turn a full circle as he stood deep in the crowd now, making eye contact with everyone who would meet his gaze. "Volunteers to the main gates in ten minutes," he called loudly, "and we can all forget this shitty day."

He turned to walk away before a voice stopped him.

"What about the prisoners?"

He stopped, turning back to the source of the question to find himself looking at a boy on the verge of needing to shave properly.

"Prisoners?" Xavier asked him.

"You've taken my father prisoner," the young man said indignantly.

"And he will have the chance to come with us and redeem himself," Xavier responded flatly, turning away and nodding to Jean-Pierre, who tossed him the fire axe he had chosen to take outside the fence with him.

———

Xavier had doubts about how many people would show up. He had convinced himself that these people were ungrateful. They'd been saved by him and his crew, along with those dock workers stranded inside the fences, back when it all started so suddenly, and now they were happy to let others do the dangerous work on their behalf.

Almost fifty people, a quarter of the total they had there, arrived carrying empty bags and wielding various melee weapons adapted or repurposed to crush skulls. Xavier couldn't believe it, but Jean-Pierre made no attempt to hide his smug grin.

"You see, Captain?" he said as he beamed a smile of bright, white teeth at him, "I told you that going out would be a good idea. It seems like I am not the only one to think this."

Xavier said nothing. He chose four of his men, trusted among his entire crew, and asked them to stay behind and man the gates. They were unhappy with their orders, because there was no mistake that when the captain asked them to do something, it didn't come with an option of saying no. But Xavier gave them reassurance that he needed good men at the gates that he could rely on them to make sure that their escape was well protected.

"And remember," he told them conspiratorially, "if anyone

looks like they... like they aren't themselves... then you know what to do, right?"

They understood.

Xavier climbed up on a stack of crates, axe in one hand and the other held up for quiet.

"Everybody works in pairs," he told them, "never leave your back unprotected. Grab everything you can carry and get back here. What we find goes into one stockpile and everybody gets fed."

"That's bollocks," shouted a voice nearby, "if we're risking our necks, then we get to keep what we find."

Xavier fixed the speaker with a look.

"If that's how you want to be, then yous can fucking stay out there, do you understand me?"

The man quailed under the sudden anger, unwilling to risk calling the man's bluff.

"There's young kids back there," Xavier said, "women with little ones. Old folks. You want them to fetch their own stuff? Is that who we are?"

The low mumbles had the vague tone of agreement, so Xavier jumped down again and nodded to his men to haul back the gates.

They spilled into the wide, fog-filled street separating the docks from the city, splitting off in different directions so as not to move as a single crowd like locusts. Jean-Pierre naturally had his captain's back, as he expected the bearded Liverpudlian to have his, and both turned right to jog down the deserted street towards the nearest shops.

None of the creatures came for them. In fact, none of them were even visible on the streets, which filled them all with an elative hope bordering on over-confident.

Just because we haven't seen any yet doesn't mean they aren't there, Xavier told himself.

And he had no idea how right he was.

He approached the large, single-storey building with Jean-Pierre jogging beside him. The noise of their breathing was rapid and ragged, and clouds of condensation lingered around their heads when they paused at a junction. They had gone south, directly away from the docks, and found themselves in an area which seemed run down even before the world had stopped turning months before. A crowd of maybe twenty others had followed in their footsteps, despite his instructions for everyone to split up into pairs and not cluster together to attract attention. He mentally shrugged, knowing that he couldn't think for everyone, and glanced at Jean-Pierre to see the man squinting ahead into the fog.

"Costco," he said simply.

"Perfect," Captain Xavier replied, "that will do us."

They went in fast, the crowd behind them speeding up when they saw that the two men had a clear goal in mind, and the sliding metal frame doors were forced open with a dozen hands working their way into the gaps. They poured inside, packets being torn open and precious contents spilled onto the floor despite his words. He was more annoyed that none of them seemed to be awake to any potential risks and instead just blindly ran in to grab armfuls of food packets and tins.

"Use your brains," he yelled as loudly as he dared, "get some bloody shopping trolleys and load it up properly."

Some of them stopped, regarding him with full mouths as their senses returned. They did so, sanity restoring the group as though it passed from person to person like another infection. Despite the growl in his stomach, he kept both hands on his axe as he watched over the now orderly emptying of shelves. Racks of cans and packets were cleared, and his spirits lifted as he knew he would eventually see the winter through without any more outbreaks of civil disobedience or starvation. He relaxed enough to start helping load the supplies himself, slipping the axe through the loop of his belt, which he loosened for the purpose, and used both hands to grab the food which would mean their survival.

A scream, more of a strangled yell from the throat of a man making an involuntary noise tore the air. Mike Xavier dropped the pallets of beans he held and fumbled to free the axe which was caught in his clothing. He took his eyes away from the source of the noise for long enough to pull it clear, only to look ahead and see a door at the rear of the shop being held open by a small procession of dead bastards. A feeling of cold dread descended through his body, slowing time and his reactions to a deathly speed, but allowing his brain to savour every moment of terror. The smell hit him; dry and musty like rotten meat left out to dry. The grey pallor of them sickened him, like the bodies he had seen retrieved from the docks in the past with clear, bloated skin. He felt his feet moving forwards before his mind realised he had commanded his body to respond to the threat.

The first savage swing of the axe was wild and while full of raw power, it was poorly aimed. With a shout of pure rage and fear, the wide blade buried itself into the skull of the first zombie in line and stuck fast, toppling his victim but taking his weapon away in the same action. The falling body did nothing to slow the three behind it as they fanned out in a perfectly orchestrated flanking move and forced him backwards away from their grasp. He tripped on the man who had screamed first, landing on top of him as their legs tangled, and both looked up at their impending deaths with looks of open-mouthed horror. Mike Xavier, captain of his beloved *Maggie* and beloved leader of his crew, closed his eyes as he knew he had failed them all.

A curious sound made his eyes open again. It was the hollow, echoing sound of metal connecting with bone, and it was answered with the cruel crunch of one of those things giving way to the force of the other. Xavier looked up to see Jean-Pierre drawing himself up to his full height, adding a little more with his raised tiptoes, as his hands were behind his back to bring the heavy metal spike back down in a woodchopper's strike to pummel and destroy the skull of the nearest zombie with such savagery that the thing was almost decapitated.

Jean-Pierre's exposed skin on his face beaded with sweat, making his forehead glisten in the poor light of the shop. He raised the long metal spike again, turning his body sideways to swing it like a baseball bat at the final zombie left standing, dealing it a brutally savage blow which snapped the head back unnaturally. Slowly, horrifyingly, the head rotated back to look at him and revealed a gruesomely dislocated jaw. The obvious injury didn't stop the thing, didn't slow it down or register any pain on its expressionless face. Jean-Pierre, exhausted after the incredible physical effort put into the three massive blows, kicked the thing in the chest to give himself space from it. Xavier scrambled to his feet, using the man he had fallen on as a tool to push himself up, and not caring, he snatched at the handle of the axe still embedded in the skull of the first dead zombie. He placed the sole of his left boot on the face, feeling the nose give way under the pressure as he pushed, and split open the top of the skull like a boiled egg as the blade broke free. Instead of luxuriously yellow yolk spilling out, a foul-smelling and gelatinous chunk of grey brain matter flopped onto the ground beside his foot and threatened to void the bile from his stomach in an instant.

He gathered himself, spun the axe so that the pointed section instead of the wide blade was pointing forwards, and swung to impale the kneeling thing in the part where the neck met the head.

It stiffened, lifeless the second the cruel, cold metal punctured the dead flesh, and it flopped to the deck.

Xavier met Jean-Pierre's eyes as the two men stood panting for breath.

"Everybody grab what you've got," Xavier shouted, bending to help up the man he had fallen over, "and get back to the docks. Now."

He propelled the man forwards and turned to face the door where the attack had come from. Jean-Pierre stood at his side and both men felt the gathering tension build to the point where the two of them felt the urge, the pathological need, to turn and run.

Nothing came, and they backed out of the shop together as their boots kicked at fallen and discarded packets littering the floor. The last man out before them was the one who had tripped him inadvertently.

"You alright?"

"Yeah," the man gasped as he held his right arm as if his shoulder was injured, "I'll be okay…"

Xavier pushed the man ahead of him, not seeing how he quickly pulled back the sleeve of his coat to look at the neat oval of puncture marks on his wrist. The bleeding had stopped almost instantly, and the heat he was feeling was close to unbearable. Terrified that he would be left outside the safety of the docks, he kept his mouth shut and staggered to keep up with the others heading back towards safety, or at least what they all thought was safety.

ELEVEN

Bill Hampton, the still-limping sergeant of marines, was on watch when the van pulled back into sight of their small village enclave. He waited for confirmation, not wanting to open up their defences without knowing that it was indeed his people driving and that none of them were infected, before pushing aside the barricade to allow them inside. That confirmation was given by Johnson leaning his head out of the window and giving a thumbs-up gesture, which Hampton took as the universal sign language for everything being hunky-dory.

It wasn't, obviously, and the looks on their faces told him that everything was not right in the world. Worse than the usual amount of not right, anyway.

"What's happened?" Bill asked, his eyes scanning to double check that everyone who went out came back whole.

"Get everyone inside first," Johnson told him, handing him a heavy bag stuffed full of shotgun cartridges which weighed him down in an instant. They went inside, heavy coats being stripped off as the interior was warm by comparison to the bitter outside temperatures. The bags and gun cases were laid down, and Kimberley walked from the kitchen wearing a smile of relief and genuine happiness that they were back. That smile, just as Hampton's had, faded in an instant as she read their faces.

"What's happened?" she asked, her own eyes scanning the returning faces to make sure everyone had come back.

"Come and sit down, please," Johnson said in a curious tone of voice that, if his men had heard him speak with it, would make them think that he had gone soft. Something about her disarmed him.

Peter walked in through the front door and laid down his weapon, his suspicious eyes betraying that he knew something was wrong. Johnson expected him to ask the question too, but he merely shrugged off his oversized coat and sat down to wait for the news.

Astrid rummaged in a bag, coming out with a large rectangular black plastic case and offering it to Peter with a smile.

"There was not much that I could find," she explained, "but I see the *Care Bears* movie and I say to myself that Amber would like this, no?"

Peter smiled, taking it from her with a nod and running up the stairs, no doubt to put it on in the big bedroom for her. That fact alone spoke volumes about the people who had owned that house; the fact that they had a VCR and a TV in their bedroom meant that they probably had too much money to spend.

Kimberley had made a large pot of tea as soon as she'd heard their return and had set it down with the cups on the coffee table by the time Peter returned. Some of the adults exchanged looks, but Johnson and Bufford both shrugged at each other as if to say that they wouldn't keep the boy out of the loop anyway. Amber was different, but this little lad had the mind of a thirty-year-old when it came to practical matters.

"We cleared a gun shop quite satisfactorily," Johnson

started, pouring himself a mug of black tea and dropping in two sugar lumps from the bowl beside the pot, "and most of a grocery shop too before we heard noises."

"What kind of noises?" Kimberley asked eagerly, stalling the telling of the story and delaying it. The others, being all forces personnel, knew when to ask questions and when to shut up and listen. So too, it seemed, did Peter.

"Gunfire and engines. Military vehicles, but not ours. I'm certain of that."

"They fired at me," Enfield said without indignation or anger in his voice, just the facts of the matter. Hampton frowned. Kimberley gave a small gasp and Peter furrowed his brow as though trying to understand why anyone living would do that. He reached the answer quickly, as the majority of his experiences with other survivors were negative until he had met his current company.

"Who?" Hampton asked.

"Why?" Kimberley chimed in at the same time.

"Who is uncertain, other than the fact that one of them was on the island with us. That means that he either got separated from the main group or he chose to leave," he explained, leaving out the name of his nemesis in case he betrayed how angry he was, "As for why, I can only assume they either thought Enfield was a dead 'un, which is unlikely seeing as he was running and carrying a gun, or they just don't like people seeing their business. Either way, we don't want to meet them again."

"So, what do we do?" Hampton asked.

"We need to join up with the others again," Johnson said, seeing nods of agreement ripple around the small group, "but I don't see how we can find them until this bloody weather has passed."

"Which will be many weeks yet, I think," Astrid chimed in.

Silence descended on them, broken only by Peter struggling

to pour himself a cup of black tea. Nobody moved to help him, signifying that they respected his independence and not that they didn't care for him, and he sat back down to sip the hot liquid before offering his own opinion.

"There can't be that many places they could be, surely?" his little eyes searched the assembled faces looking at him, "I mean, I don't really know, but seeing as they are soldiers too, wouldn't they think the same as you and find somewhere that they could stay?"

The adults exchanged looks. The concept was nothing really new to them, but hearing it come from his mouth made it a little more real in the moment. Truth be told, they had been busy concentrating on surviving and consolidating more than they had been thinking about searching for the rest of the survivors from the island.

"That's true," Kimberley said, "where would you take your people if you were in that position?"

Bufford looked at Johnson. He had been in that position; however, it had been in the hands of his captain and not the senior NCO, and he had only known part of the working logic at the time.

"We need maps," he said, "and we can try to work out where they would have gone. We can also see about more supplies."

"I'll get on it," Bufford said as he glanced to Astrid. She nodded her assent that she would help.

"So, what did you get today?" Hampton asked, changing the subject.

"New toys," Johnson answered, standing to fetch his new shotgun and handing it over for inspection.

"Nice," the old sergeant said with relish, "universal door opener."

"Exactly," Johnson answered, seeing Peter's curious gaze at the weapon. He knew the boy had his own gun, one that he had even modified by taking off the barrels and stock to make it small enough for him to carry and use. He had only pulled the trigger once, he had told him, but for such a young boy to have decapitated an enemy with a shotgun and be alright with it signified something of a change in the way they viewed children.

Enfield stood too, retrieving the gun slips and producing the big hunting rifle first and the small Ruger after.

"Plenty of bullets for these, too," their sniper said.

"That looks a little, um..." Kimberley said, searching for the right word which wouldn't cause offence, "small?"

"It'll do fine for popping heads at medium range," Enfield said, "plus it's very quiet."

"Quiet is good," Peter said, feeling suddenly embarrassed as they all turned to look at him. "I mean," he began, his face flushing with colour, "it's just better to not be heard is all I'm saying..."

"No," Astrid said, "Peter is correct in what he says. Quiet is indeed good."

Peter smiled and relaxed a little, the worry of giving his opinion in front of these big and frightening people washing away and being replaced with something else which he hadn't experienced before.

Acceptance? Pride? Belonging?

What he felt was totally alien to him, but he couldn't explain the main reason he was afraid to give his opinion in front of them. It was because he had lived his whole life in fear of being struck without warning if he spoke when his parents had decided that he shouldn't. The only problem with that was that he never knew when he was to stay silent until the first smack made contact with his skull. It was the reason he never stood within arm's reach of a grown up when they spoke, even if none of them noticed. It was the reason he flinched at unexpected noises and movements. It was the reason he could read the temperature and mood of a room in seconds.

Peter was a survivor. He wasn't born as such, but his life had moulded him into one. It had shaped him and trained him to be almost perfectly developed to survive the world as it now was. He was empathic to the point of being a chameleon; able to blend into invisibility just to stay safe.

"Of course he's right," Hampton said as he gave the boy a gentle pat on the shoulder with a meaty hand larger than the boy's head, "wish we'd always had officers as smart as Peter here." He beamed a smile at the boy who, for the first time in his life hadn't flinched away from being touched by an adult. Peter smiled back.

"So where do we look?" Johnson said aloud to himself. Bufford got up, sifting through the paper maps on the shelves before grabbing a few and turning back to them.

"Grab a map and start looking," he told them.

"Pete," Enfield said as he leaned over the side of his chair to pick up the new rifle, "let's leave them to it. You can help me sight this in if you like?"

Peter nodded, hiding the wider smile he felt creeping out from inside him as his brain tried to reign in his enthusiasm. He had never looked forward to anything before, never got excited about anything promised unless it was actually happening. Every so often, when one of his parents was drunk to the point of feeling magnanimous, he would be promised something that he wanted only for it to be forgotten about entirely when sobriety returned. On the rare occasions he had reminded them about such promises he had invited punishment or humiliation, so he had just given up looking forward to anything.

Walking beside the tall Royal Marine whose footsteps seemed to make no noise, his eyes kept darting to the short rifle he carried as the bubbling excitement of all young boys when given the chance to play with guns rose closer to the surface. He looked up at Enfield as they walked. The marine was twice his size but about the same relative build, which made him wonder how he had become a marine because they were supposed to be very strong and tough. He didn't know how to ask the question, mostly because he didn't know how Enfield would respond, so instead he asked what he needed him to do to help.

"I need you to spot for me," Enfield told him, producing a small set of binoculars from a webbing pouch and handed them down to him, "I need you to call out whether I'm left or right, up or down on the target."

"What target?" Peter asked, his own feet travelling at a relative velocity of three to one to maintain the same pace.

"I've got one," Enfield told him, "we just need something static to fix it to."

He led them to the far end of the village, the one from which they didn't regularly drive in and out of, and he reached into the bag he was carrying to produce three white cardboard boxes, which rattled and a handful of small, black metal rectangles.

"These are the magazines," he told Peter, "twenty rounds apiece, and they go in like this." He picked up a short bullet from the box he'd flipped open and spun it in his hands so that the brass glittered in the dull daylight before he slid it into the recess and pressed it down with his thumb. Then he added another on top. "That's two. Eighteen more."

Peter nodded, his tongue protruding slightly from one side of his mouth as he concentrated, and he carefully loaded in more bullets as Enfield spoke.

"This doesn't have a bolt, so I can't bore-sight it first. That's when you take the bolt out and line up the hole through the barrel with the target. After that you line up the sight and fire a shot." He rested the gun over a sturdy wooden fence and brought out a contraption from the bag. He rested it over the barrel and twisted the end until the G-clamp held the barrel tight to the fence. Enfield looked along the length of the barrel and squinted, pointing it at a tree about fifty paces away.

"Stay here and watch my back?"

Peter met his eye and nodded, unsure what he would do if something happened when he was outside the safety of the barricades. Enfield climbed over, still barely making a sound as he moved like the adult version of Peter, and trotted away over the cold ground. He stopped at the tree, producing a rough-torn square of beige cardboard, bearing concentric circles around a solid central circle, and held it against the trunk of the tree before tapping at the corners with something. He scanned around before jogging back, skipping over the barricade with the faintest of protests from the springs of the car he mounted as he crossed it. Looking back at his work, he squinted again and nodded to himself. Peter looked at the makeshift target, seeing that the circles were almost the same size as Enfield's head had been when he was there, and he asked about it.

"Where did you get the target?"

"It's off the side of the ration packs," Enfield told him softly, "thoughtful of them to give us food wrapped in a target. Right," the marine sniper told the boy as he bent to the rifle and changed the subject, "watch that target and tell me where the bullet hits."

Peter raised the binoculars ready but still jumped in fright when the small rifle coughed and spat a bullet far sooner than he expected. He thought that it would take time to line up a shot like that, that it would need careful consideration, but the man just aimed and shot.

"Well?" Enfield asked after a brief pause.

"Oh," Peter said hurriedly, "err, up and right?"

"How much by?" Enfield asked confusing him, as he could surely see the same thing through his scope.

"Um, like the same as my hand?"

"Flat hand or your fist?" Enfield asked him, condensing the boy's information and teaching him how to describe it.

"A fist."

"Good," Enfield said, standing up and clicking the dials on the scope before bending his head back to the sight and twisting the clamp a little tighter to make sure the gun didn't move when he fired it, "standby. Firing."

The gun spat again, no rolling echo of the gunshot rippling across the landscape as he would expect from gunfire out in the open.

"You hit the black bit," he told Enfield.

"Smack in the middle?"

"No… just above it."

"On the centre line though?"

Peter looked hard as he thought about his answer. "Slightly up from the middle. Half a fist."

Enfield made another adjustment and fired another shot, this one hitting dead centre.

"Bullseye!" Peter said, a little more loudly and excitedly than he meant to.

Enfield just smiled at him from the corner of his mouth in a cocky way as he spun the lever to release the G-clamp and free the gun.

"Now we see if that's right," he said, hefting the little rifle into his shoulder and leaning into the standing shooting position before squeezing off half a dozen shots in rapid succession. He stopped firing, looking down at Peter who still stared up at him.

"Well?"

Peter fumbled with the binoculars to look at the tree. As the picture came into focus, he saw that the very centre of the black spot was a single ragged hole exposing flashes of damaged bark and the white of virgin wood beneath.

"Whoa…"

Enfield chuckled, lowering the rifle and dropping out the spent magazine before offering it to the boy.

"Your turn," he said, seeing the glisten of happy tears in Peter's eyes staring up at him.

TWELVE

"Who the hell was it, then?" Nevin asked Michaels angrily.

"What does it matter?" he responded, pausing halfway through pouring the rusty liquid from a crystal decanter into a matching tumbler. He waved the decanter by the neck to emphasise his point and added, "Why can't you just let it go?"

Nevin said nothing, chewing at his lip instead of answering.

"Ah," Michaels said annoyingly, pausing again to take a gulp of the whisky before he went on, "you're worried about it being our former colleagues, aren't you?"

Again, Nevin said nothing, which was an answer in itself.

"Look," Michaels told him as he slumped into the leather chair by the fire, "chances are that they..." a knock at the door stopped his words as both men stared at the doorway. Their eyes followed the path of the young girl carrying a wicker basket full of logs over to the fire, with difficulty because of the weight. She dumped it down, readjusting it to keep it clear of the direct heat, then turned to give an overly sarcastic bow before she walked towards the door. Her actions showed defer-ence, but her eyes promised a painful death if only she could manage it somehow. Both men shuddered internally, privately, at seeing how much she detested them.

Michaels looked at the fire, then at the new supply of logs, then glanced pointedly at Nevin and raised an eyebrow. Nevin returned his gaze for a few beats before letting out an exasperated sigh of defeat and putting down his own glass to bend and pick up a log before tossing it half-heartedly onto the flames. Michaels tutted but carried on.

"Chances are, they are either gone or are too far away to be encroaching. It was probably just another nobody, so don't worry about it."

"Easier said than done," Nevin said, "I can't imagine they'd be happy to see me if our paths crossed again."

"Why?"

Nevin hesitated. He still hadn't revealed the full extent of his betrayal when he had fired through his own men and caused the mother of all explosions. He didn't know how many of them had survived, if any, and if any of them had, then his name would be shit among the squadron. And with the Royal Marines. And the Royal Air Force helicopter crews. And the SAS and the SBS and the civilians. It wasn't a list of enemies he wanted to think about for long, not if he wanted to sleep ever again.

"It doesn't matter," he said, "what do we do next?"

"Do?" Michaels asked after a hefty gulp of scotch and the ensuing grimace, "About what?"

"About who is out there?"

"It doesn't matter who is out there," Michaels said, his tone mocking and derogatory, "so stop flapping your bloody gums about it. We carry on as we are, we try not to freeze or starve over winter, we collect the rents, we keep our patrols going and if we want something, then we take it. You think there's a government coming back? You think we're expecting the Americans to roll in with tanks to help us out? Wake up, man. They'll be too busy keeping the outbreak firmly on this side of the Atlantic. After that, they'll be busting their guts trying to keep it from crossing the Pacific. Nobody cares about us, get it into your head."

———

Jessica kept her mouth tightly shut the entire time she was walking out of the main house. She walked slowly, taking measured steps with a neutral look on her face so that nobody knew how much she was seething. She walked tall, her head held high and her jaw set tight, and went straight back to the crowded room that she shared with the two women. The older one of them wasn't there when she walked through the door, but the young woman was. She was lying back on the bed she occupied, her head in a book, and she looked up, puzzled as Jessica fast-walked in and threw herself face down onto the pillow on her bed. She drew in a muffled breath, filling her lungs to their full capacity, and she screamed as loud and long and hard as she could.

Ellie watched her as she fully extinguished the first scream and drew in a second breath, like water withdrawing from a beach ahead of a tsunami. Despite the muffling of the pillow, the second scream was still loud enough to hurt her ears in the small confines of their room. Ellie waited for it to subside, lowering her book and breathing in to make her own sound and ask if the girl was alright. Before she could ask, a third muted scream tore the room in two and made her wince until the sound faded away to nothing.

As suddenly as the invasive sound had started, it ended, and the girl sat up to wipe the tears from her face.

"You alright, my sweet?" Ellie asked the girl. Jessica looked at her, wearing a face that said she most definitely wasn't alright, but it also seemed resigned to the fate that she was powerless to escape.

Escape, she thought, *I need to escape.*

"I'm fine," she said instead, "just angry at them."

"Which 'them'?" Ellie asked with a small smile.

"The 'alive' them. The ones who keep saying how they are 'keeping us safe'." She added emphasis to the words with scorn, which went some way to masking how scared and helpless she felt because of them. Ever since the nurse had unstrapped her from that hospital bed, she had vowed to always be in control of her own life. They had run, had found more terrified people also running, had managed to escape the hospital grounds and it felt to her as though she had been running and hiding in silence for as long as she could recall. The group she was with had changed. Some left and some joined. Others died. By the time they were 'rescued' by the people living here, she was utterly exhausted by a life on the run, and at first, she had relished sleeping for an entire day knowing that someone else was keeping watch, but after that initial elation she quickly recognised that something was very wrong.

For the second time in a month she had been effectively kidnapped and imprisoned, regardless of the legality or justification for either event, and now found herself put to work as a servant in return for a safe place to sleep and some food. They treated her like a dumb child, even more so when they saw the scars and fresher cuts on her wrists and arms, but they didn't know who or what she had been before. They didn't know she had been raising her younger brother and saw the world not like the dumb kid they assumed her to be, but like a shrewd and suspicious adult.

Ellie's own face descended into a mask of neutral hostility. The same bastards the new girl was raging about had taken her away from her daughter, knocked her out cold to stop her struggling before she could say that her baby was still in the house they were dragging her from. By the time she had come round and told them, their leader had sent the men straight back but they had found nobody. Her baby was gone; her little Amber, so innocent and such a good girl, was lost to her forever.

She had steeled herself, cloaked herself in a numbness to just wait out the storm, and when order was restored, she would tell the authorities just what these people had done, and they would be punished for it. She tried her hardest not to think about her daughter, because the thoughts paralysed her. She had no tears left, no more capacity for anger, just the flickering pilot light of survival that kept her burning at the lowest possible setting.

As selfish as she felt, she could offer Jessica no solace or agreement and talk about these people and what they had done to them. Jessica knew all about Ellie's story, told to her by Pauline, who shared the room with them, but ripping off the scabs of someone else was a cruel thing to do. She knew that the woman missed her child, just as she missed Peter terribly and broke down every time she imagined him being left behind. Her thoughts of him suffering at the hands of this new world weren't the worst thing she could imagine, but instead her anger and fear was that he had been left in the dubious care of their parents. She shuddered to think what would happen to him if he'd been left alone with them, but she knew that a violent death at the hands and teeth of the monsters that normal people had become would probably be a blessing.

"I miss my brother," she told Ellie in a quiet voice, "and I don't know who would have looked after him when I wasn't there."

"How old was he?" Elie asked in a matching low tone.

"He *is* three years younger than me. He'll be ten now."

Ellie bit her lip, not realising she had spoken as though her brother was already dead. He probably was, but that kind of realistic pessimism wouldn't have gone down well with her.

"What about your parents? Grandparents?"

Jessica scoffed and curled a lip in disgust. "We didn't have much use for them even before this. He was left alone with them, which is worse than being properly alone."

"What do you mean?" Ellie asked, sitting forward and feeling suddenly heartbroken for the girl and her missing brother.

"Every day," she said dully, her eyes unfocused and staring at a blank spot on the wall, "we wouldn't know what mood she was in. I'd get him up and get him dressed, I'd feed him breakfast and we'd go to school before she woke up. Our father was already out, gone to work still drunk usually, so we just learned to take care of ourselves. When it wasn't a school day we would do the same. Sometimes I'd still make us packed lunches and we would go off for the day. The punishments for disappearing weren't as bad as if we'd stayed there anyway. She would hit us, then wait until he got back in from work on the farm, and then she'd make up lies about how bad we had been. He would hit us and he never once believed us that she had already dished out the smacks." She took an exaggerated sigh, as though the memories coming back to her were exhausting. "There was a stick, a thin walking stick, that they hung on the wall outside our bedrooms. It was our reminder to do everything right and stay out of their way. When it came down it…" she closed her eyes and lowered her gaze, "…it wasn't a good place to be, and I left him there. I need to go back and find him."

Ellie bit her lip again. She wanted to say that he wouldn't be there. That no child that young could survive on their own, even if they'd had a good start in life, which these two obviously hadn't. She said nothing, because the girl needed something to believe in. It was at that moment, right then as she watched the girl's face turn from catatonic exhaustion to angry resolve, that she knew she had given up too soon on her own child. With a surge of heat that seemed to run through her body and electrify her, she sat up, energised, and grabbed the girl by both shoulders.

"Snap out of it," she told her with a gentle shake, "we can get through this. We can get out of here and we can find them."

"How?" Jessica asked, looking up at her with something resembling hope breaking through the tiredness. Just then the door opened and Pauline stood there, wearing a curious look as she took in the two of them locked in their intense conversation.

"Maybe Pauline can help us," Ellie said hopefully.

THIRTEEN

Captain Palmer walked through the woods behind their large house with Major Downes. The two men had a respect for each other that had grown to be something resembling a friendship, but each was closely committed to their tasks and didn't lose time on frivolities. That said, both understood that taking the time to keep themselves sane was just as important as staying fit and healthy.

They had taken their breakfast together, enjoying the wholesome goodness of warm, fresh bread to accompany the eggs and the meagre ration of a single slice of bacon, and at the invitation of Downes, Palmer had joined him to investigate the reports of deer seen close to the house. Hunting animals with military weaponry may not have been sporting, but meat was meat and they had little time to observe the niceties. Downes, much to Smiffy's sullen disgust, had borrowed his stolen soviet sniper rifle and loaned the tank captain his own MP5 so that neither of their shots would be heard far away. The pretence of hunting deer was no fallacy, but Downes wanted Palmer well away from any other ears before he told him the facts he had yet to share with anyone outside of his own patrol. Those men could be trusted to keep their mouths shut, as could Palmer, he suspected, but the man was under a lot of other conflicting pressures and his reaction was less than a certainty.

"How are we looking for winter?" Downes asked, hoping that Palmer would suggest that their current position was untenable.

"We seem to have broken the back of it," he said almost happily, "if we can just get through the worst of this winter, then we should be well on our way to rebuilding."

Downes kept his voice low and his eyes ahead, as the intelligence regarding the deer was genuine.

"Given the choice," he said carefully, "would you want to rejoin any other units left alive?"

Palmer stopped and looked directly at the SAS Major.

"Who and where?" Palmer shot back, seeing through the uncharacteristically clumsy attempt at hypothesis.

Downes took one look at the younger man's face and decided not to lie to him. He just had to trust that he would do the right thing with the full facts.

"Inner Hebrides. Part of the Doomsday protocol was for special forces to take as many surviving members of government as possible to a safe location."

Palmer thought about it for a moment before asking, "Major, do we still have a working government?"

"I'm not sure about working, but yes. We still have cabinet members alive and protected."

"Major," Palmer said just as carefully, "why did you keep this information from me until now?"

"Julian," Downes said in an apologetic tone, "please understand that this was part of the wider picture that I wasn't at liberty to discu…"

"God dammit, Major!" Palmer erupted, "you think I have enjoyed thinking that we are all that is left? You think I have relished the thought of turning farmer and becoming the bloody mayor instead of a soldier? Damn you, Major," he cursed without the full force of his opening words, "and to answer your question I would rejoin in a heartbeat."

"I only had this confirmed yesterday," Downes told him, "and I apologise for not telling you before. So how do we do this?"

"We go there, Major, immediately."

"And how do we transport all of our personnel, the civilians, and our equipment there?" Downes countered.

"I shall speak with Lieutenant Commander Barrett, and see if we can manage relay flights," Palmer said.

"That's a possibility, but it's doubtful. I would suggest that the safest option would be a road convoy."

"In this weather?" Palmer asked.

"It may be slower and less comfortable, but air is less certain. I doubt Harry would want to run those kinds of relays. It's maybe four hundred and fifty miles as the crow flies."

"That gets him there and less than halfway back on a full tank, which he doesn't have. Another refuelling trip?"

"It's possible," Downes said, "I know they have a very small airfield up there, but perhaps using the helicopter for precious cargo and as many of the civilians as possible would be better?"

Both men lapsed into silence as they ran through their own private thoughts and plans until a snapping sound brought them back to the present. Neither men instinctively recalled the deer they were after and both were alert for the screeching, shuffling onslaught of rotting people. For them to see the dusky speckled fawn directly ahead of them was a pleasant surprise. They froze, both slowly raising their guns.

"Take the shot if you please, Major," Palmer whispered. Downes said nothing but carried on the slow movements to bring the VAL into his shoulder. A soft click sounded, then the tiny atmospheric change as he held his breath in anticipation of the shot, then the sharp metallic snap of the action firing.

The deer fell, making both men smile in anticipation of fresh meat, but it seemed as though they weren't the only ones stalking the animal, as another sound ripped through the air in answer. Downes, still looking through the scope at the fallen animal, twitched the scope upwards to the frost-covered features of an old man advancing towards them. Its wild eyebrows twitched above the milky eyes, focused as much as they could be on the fallen animal and not on them. Downes held his shot, scanning around, and counted three more advancing from the same direction.

"Advance left flank twenty metres," Downes said in a low voice, totally professional in an instant, "four enemy ahead."

Palmer moved low, disciplined enough not to run and make more noise to attract their attention to him. Behind to his right came the steady, rhythmic sounds of more sharp snaps as Downes began putting fat, sub-sonic 9mm bullets into rotten and frozen skulls. Palmer drew level with their kill, raising the borrowed MP5 and drilling a three-round burst into the side profile of a woman reaching out for the warm corpse of the deer.

"Fuck it," he snarled, abnormally savage with his language but justified as he saw the rough chunk of flesh torn from the animal's back. He looked for more targets, wanting to kill more of them for contaminating their meat and ruining the day.

"Withdraw," Downes called out, prompting the captain to turn away and thread his way back through the trees.

"Where the bloody hell did they come from?" he asked as he fell in beside the Major in their retreat.

"They're everywhere," Downes said. "Have you noticed it's warmer under the tree cover?"

He had, although he hadn't made the connection between

that slight temperature increase and the faster movement of the Screechers.

"Would you prefer a Scottish island?" Downes asked him.

"Yes, Major, yes I would."

————

"Send it, Smiffy," Downes said to his man on the complex radio set. The burst transmission, already typed in and ready to send, shot up into the ether as a high-frequency data burst.

ECHO-ONE-ONE, CHARLIE-ONE-ONE. STATE AVAILABILITY OF AVIA-TION FUEL ON YOUR END. SINGLE HELICOPTER AVAILABLE BUT INSUFFICIENT FUEL FOR MORE THAN ONE SORTIE. INTENT TO TRAVEL BY ROAD. ADVISE.

They sat in silence, waiting for any response to come and knowing that it could be up to twelve hours later, depending on any number of varying factors. Palmer had joined them in their small den, which was deemed out of bounds for anyone but the enigmatic men from Hereford. Lloyd was with them, invited into the folds of secrecy out of necessity and trust on Palmer's behalf. What wasn't odd in the slightest was the lack of the presence of the half-mad Colonel and the younger brother of the captain, a constant source of embarrassment to him. To their relief, a responding transmission came in quickly.

CHARLIE-ONE-ONE, ECHO-ONE-ONE. MINIMAL STOCKS OF FUEL, HELICOPTER A NO-GO. BY ROAD, RV 57.003813N, 5.8271730W. TRANSPORT PROVIDED BY FERRY. GOD SPEED.

. . .

"Mac?" Downes said.

"Go," the Scotsman answered, grabbing a pad and pencil. Downes recounted the grid coordinates and heard the responding scratch of lead on paper.

"Give me a minute," Mac said as he pulled open a map. Palmer turned to Lloyd, who had cleared his throat to offer a suggestion.

"If Harry and James could fly the civvies up," he said, meaning Lieutenant Commander Barrett and his junior co-pilot Lieutenant Morris, "then that leaves us with a combined forces strength of what? Forty men left? Two trucks, supplies, at least one or two of the Foxes?"

"Got it," Mac cut in, "Mallaig. It'll be the ferry port to Skye, I wager."

"You'd want to convoy for what, seven hundred miles?" Downes asked Lloyd after turning back from his sergeant.

"What other choice do we have?" the marine lieutenant answered.

"None," Palmer said, "not unless we stay here and wait to starve or be overrun. I, gentlemen, would much prefer to have a small stretch of the North Atlantic between us and the Screechers."

"So, Captain," Downes asked formally, "how do we convince the civilians to go?"

"We need more food first," Palmer said tiredly.

———

The small collection of officers and soldiers weren't the only ones huddled in a room too small for them and planning a way out. Miles away, on the cliffs above the foaming white crashes of waves far below, sat a young girl and two women speaking in low voices to one another.

"It would be better to leave either at night or very early," Pauline said to the others, "most of them will be asleep."

"The guards never sleep," Ellie offered darkly, her eyes unfocused and distant in thought. "They would if we made them, though…"

"What do you mean?" Jessica asked. Ellie didn't answer her directly, instead she turned to Pauline intently and asked her a question.

"Can you steal a bottle of alcohol? Something strong?"

Pauline thought about it for a long moment before nodding slowly with a sceptical look in her eye. "What are you thinking?"

"It would look too obvious if we just walked up to one of the guards and gave them a bottle, wouldn't it?" she asked, explaining her plan through the medium of asking rhetorical questions to lead them through each step, "so how about one of us gets caught near the guards and we make it look like we're trying to *hide* the bottle? That way they'll just take it off us and send us away. Then we wait and slip past them after they've drunk it."

"Won't work," Pauline said flatly, disappointment heavy in her tone, "because they change the guards halfway through the night. I've seen it. They'd probably just wait for a few hours, then go and drink it when they get back inside. Michaels is pretty hot on that kind of thing…"

Ellie sat back, all enthusiasm gone in an instant to be replaced with sullen defeat. The three of them sat in silence for a while before the girl spoke.

"We need a diversion," she said in a small voice, her eyes only raised to meet theirs after she had spoken.

"Like what?" Ellie asked.

"A fire," said Pauline distantly, "fire always gets people scared and running around."

"So what do we set on fire?" Ellie asked.

"Nevin," Jessica answered nastily, an evil curl on her lip as she spoke the name of the horrible man who humiliated her.

The older women didn't know whether to laugh or be scared.

"Our bedding," Pauline offered, "throw it out of the window here after it's on fire and that way they'll have to go around the building to see where it's coming from. They sat in silence for a while, each of them considering the plausibility of the plan.

"It could work," Ellie said as she narrowed her eyes, "but has anyone got a lighter?"

Pauline and Ellie exchanged looks and shrugs, and a resigned huff from the girl made them both look in her direction. She rolled up the leg of her trousers to expose the tops of the boots she had been wearing ever since she ran from the hospital barefoot. Tucked inside the top was a lighter, beside a metal nail file, a Yale style key, and a teaspoon. Lost for words, the other two said nothing as the girl replaced the trouser leg and displayed the needed item.

"What?" she said when she saw the looks of the others, "I see things and I pick them up. You never know when they'll come in handy."

Pauline took the lighter and struck a flame with her thumb on the third attempt.

"We still need something inflammable," she said, "to make the flames nice and big."

"You're joking, right?" Ellie said, "with these mattresses?"

Pauline looked aghast at the implied criticism of the place she had lived and worked in for so long, but still didn't understand Ellie's point.

"Polyurethane foam?" Ellie asked, almost annoyed that nobody understood her point, "It's very inflammable," she finished.

Both Pauline and Jessica gave an, "ahh," in unison.

"So we set fire to the bedding, toss it out of the window, wait for everyone to start running around and then what?" Jessica asked.

"Then we make a run for it," Pauline said.

"Where?" Jessica asked.

"Anywhere," said Ellie, sounding more reckless than she truly was, "just away from here and these pigs."

"Out there," Jessica asked softly, "with the monsters?"

"Yes," she bit back, "anywhere is better than here."

FOURTEEN

"We can't stay inside forever," Hampton said through his gritted teeth as he flexed and bent his damaged leg.

"No," Johnson countered, "but neither can we risk running around in sub-freezing temperatures with snow and ice everywhere."

"We need to, Dean," Bufford said as he placed a calming hand on the man's shoulder, "if not for ourselves, then for the kids; they need more food than we have left and if we wait for the weather to get worse, the job will be much harder."

Johnson couldn't argue with the logic It wasn't as though they needed his permission anyway, he wasn't in charge of them, but it had evolved that decisions were made in a more democratic fashion than their former lives would have thought possible. None of them was placed above the others. Johnson was a very senior non-commissioned officer, but then Hampton and Bufford were both hugely experienced sergeants who had trained more than their fair share of young officers in nominal command of the men they served with. Astrid, the curious commando spy from Norway, was clearly no uniform-filler, and possessed a sometimes frightening intellect. Even their lowly-ranked marine, Enfield, was a specialist and a cunning man with an eye for ground like a predator.

Hell, Johnson thought, *even the kids are qualified to weigh in on decisions, given how long they've survived on their own.*

The only person not to hold rank or military experience was Kimberley, but something about the woman was so forthright that she was not the meek kind to simply obey orders she didn't agree with or understand. Johnson had tried, very delicately given their tenuous attraction to one another, to explain to her that if the time ever came that she was told what to do in a dire situation, then she simply had to bite her tongue and trust the people she was with. She had accepted that, but something told the big man that those were the only set of circumstances under which she would submit to rule.

"Fine," he said eventually, "what are you thinking?"

"Small recce team," Bufford said, "not looking at shops or houses but more at commercial stuff. That means," he said as he spread out a map, "heading back this way towards the coast."

Johnson looked at the map but could see no reason to refuse the man.

"You'll keep an eye out for signs of others though, correct?"

"We will. Good or bad, we'll make damned sure first," Enfield answered for the SBS man.

You've already planned who'll be going then... Johnson told himself.

"I'll come with you," he said.

"Three-man team. Small, quiet, fast," Astrid said in a tone of voice which brooked no argument.

Johnson looked at her, then Bufford, then Enfield in turn and saw no shame in their eyes. They weren't trying to circumvent him, not intentionally, and he tried to find any logical reason to force one of the three elite soldiers out of their role so that he could retain a hands-on approach. It was pointless, and he knew it. Two special forces commandos and a sniper? How could he hope to replace one of those at their job? If it was co-ordinating the resupply of an armoured squadron, then Dean Johnson was your man. Laying an ambush using his faster tracked vehicles and luring enemy tanks into a killing ground he had set up to pour murderous 40mm fire into them? That was, as they said, most definitely his bag. But running around in freezing conditions, moving like a ghost and fighting like half a platoon if called upon, then no; he was no commando.

"Timescale?" he asked, changing the subject from his dark thoughts of inadequacy.

"Leave at first light tomorrow, be back by dark," Bufford said confidently.

"Alright," Johnson said, all fight leaving him and his belly already turning towards happier thoughts, "but you really need to bring back supplies tomorrow, because you need to eat well tonight." The SBS sergeant and former Royal Marine smiled at the Squadron Sergeant Major, who thought that the muscular man had already visibly lost enough size to be a concern for them all. They had been living on reduced rations ever since their panicked return from the gun store, while fear of heavy machine gun fire kept their heads down for the ensuing weeks, until hunger promised a far crueller death. His beard, wild before their helicopter had crashed and stranded them in the countryside, had grown wispy and looked bedraggled until he took scissors to it and cut it shorter. Johnson himself, despite attempts to maintain standards for no reason other than that he had always done so, had succumbed and grown a tough, scratchy beard of short hair which came through with a ginger hue, despite his hair the being darkest of brown.

They were, he had to admit, in a bad way, and that would

only worsen if they didn't break out of hibernation and find more supplies.

But there were so many risks. The roads were iced over, after weeks of snow and frosts and thaws and more frosts. Packed snow had turned to mush, only to freeze solid and dry once more into slabs as hard as concrete which wouldn't fade under an entire day of direct sunlight. They had to be almost three months shy of the break of spring, and this winter had conspired with other events to be the worst in as long as he could recall.

The only person not bothered by the temperatures was Astrid Larsen, but then again Johnson guessed that if your home country regularly experienced minus thirty degrees inland during winter, then the constant snow and sleet of a British winter, no matter how harsh, was of little concern. What *was* concerning, at least to Johnson, was that their country was not set up for such a bad winter, just as it couldn't cope with a prolonged period of hot weather in the summer, and if the world hadn't turned into a flesh-eating circus, there would have been frozen hell on earth this winter anyway.

The cold was good for one thing though; the dead were slow, lethargic, and very few in number. Those that did wander into their little fortified island posed next to no threat, unless you fell on your arse in front of them and dropped your weapon, that was. They had all expressed a hope that the bad weather would put an end to the infected population.

"Who wants to cook then?" Hampton chimed in, making it obvious that he was hungry and wasn't going to cook.

"I'll do it," came a small voice from the open-plan kitchen behind their conversation in the comfortable lounge. Heads turned to take in the small frame of Peter, the sleeves of his oversized sweatshirt rolled up and slipping down constantly over his bony elbows as he hefted a large pasta pan into the sink and ran the tap to fill it. "Spaghetti and meatballs okay for everyone?"

They had kept the dozen tins of meatballs back intentionally, and the dried pasta was probably good for a lifetime if they weren't overly fussy, which clearly none of them was.

"Need a hand?" Kimberley asked. Peter just turned and smiled at her, so she used the can opener to wind off the jagged metal discs before pouring the lumpy, sloppy contents into another pan for heating.

"Where's Amber?" Astrid asked from the other room, seeing that the two people other than herself who the little girl gravitated to were engaged in the cooking.

"She's right here," Peter said, "she's helping me, isn't that right?" he turned to pull a face at her as she was sitting up on the kitchen worktop out of sight of the lounge area. She pulled the face back playfully, but still didn't say a word.

They ate together, testimony to the sheer size of the house as all eight of them could sit around the massive dining table set in the kitchen and still feel as though the house was empty. When they had finished, Johnson and Hampton went with the three who would be leaving in the morning, and Amber went back upstairs to watch the Care Bears movie for the third time that day. Peter, uncomplaining, took the plates and rested them in the large sink beside the pans. He shoved the sleeves of his top up his arms again, not bothering to rectify it when they slid down immediately afterwards, and he ran the tap. Kimberley got up, taking a flat sponge and holding it under the water, which had already run warm, then turned to clean down the table.

He washed, armpits resting on the sink edge and sleeves dropping into the soapy water, as she dried.

"Who taught you how to do this?" she asked, full of curiosity.

"My sister," he told her after the briefest of pauses as

though he was deciding whether to tell her or not. "She did a lot of cooking. She showed me how to cook the pasta and test it, but she didn't let me open the tins because I could cut myself on them." He left out that she liked to use the jagged slices of metal to score lines in her own arms.

"She showed me how to wash up as we went along, and she made my sandwiches for the next day as we did it."

Kimberley, her heart breaking with each word he spoke, resisted the urge to patronise him. He was clearly very resilient, and to make out that his survival was extraordinary was to invite doubt into his mind.

"Were your parents working then?" she asked, seeing the boy turn and regard her quizzically.

"No," he told her, "they watched TV and drank and smoked cigarettes. We weren't allowed to watch the TV most of the time." He went back to washing, his sponge making squeaking noises on the plate as he wiped circles of soap suds onto it. Kimberley didn't know what to say, but she found herself asking the question she knew she shouldn't.

"Peter, where is your sister now?"

He paused, thinking, then resumed the squeaking on the plate.

"She went away, to hospital, so she's probably there now. I'll try and find her after this has all finished."

Before Kimberley could even start to figure out what to say to that, Peter asked his own question.

"What happened to your face?"

She froze, hearing the question asked so blatantly and innocently when people usually never had the courage to ask her.

"It was an accident," she told him quietly, resting down one clean plate and picking up another to dry.

"Was it an accident doing a new roof?" Peter asked, "Only I saw when we had a new roof on the pig shed at home, and someone accidentally poured hot tar stuff down their hand and it looked the same.

"No, Peter, it wasn't an accident with roofing tar, it was..." she trailed off.

"What?" he asked her, a concerned look on his face as he turned to her.

"Someone hurt me," she told him, "someone I should have been safe with, but I wasn't."

"Was it your parents?" he asked, "did they hit you, too?"

"No," she said, a tear forming in her eye, not for her own mistreatment but for the terrible reality the boy had lived before zombies roamed the country, "it was my... my husband. I got married very young, you see, and he wasn't very nice to me."

"Oh," Peter said, clearly sad for her, "did you tell the police?"

"In a way," Kimberley said, snapping out of her reverie and scrubbing the tea towel at the plate once more.

"Did someone hurt him back for you?" Peter asked as he washed up.

"I did it myself," she blurted out before she could stop herself.

Peter stopped, thinking about it, then continued scrubbing. "That's good. You shouldn't let bullies keep hitting you. I did that once, hit him back, and he didn't try it again." Peter's eyes went vacant for a moment as his mind followed the logic that the bully was probably no longer alive.

Kimberley said nothing, simply put the dry plate down and folded the damp tea towel before giving the boy a gentle flat palm on the head as she turned away. She didn't trust herself to speak lest the tears come again. She hadn't talked about what had happened for years, and moving to the country had been her way of leaving it behind her, in the past with her married name.

The planning conversation had ended during the time she had been with Peter, so when she walked into what she thought was an empty room with red, puffy eyes and her chest heaving with the effort of keeping her tears at bay, she wasn't expecting to find the two men standing mutely staring at her.

"This one will be fine for me," Hampton said in a stage voice as he took the closest book to him, a hardback Catherine Cookson that didn't seem like his kind of thing at all. He made his limping escape from the room, his injured leg still rendering him less useful than he wanted to be, leaving her facing an embarrassed Dean Johnson who seemed as though he didn't know where to look.

"Um…" he started, looking left and right for escape and finding none. He began to edge away, leaving the distressed woman to cry in peace, but she threw herself down to the sofa and let out a high-pitched growl of frustration.

"I'll, err, just be going…"

"I'll be okay," she said, wiping angrily at the tears on her cheeks, "I promised myself I'd stopped crying about this years ago," she said as she waved a hand over the scarred side of her face, "but I just got reminded of something and it caught me off guard."

Johnson sat carefully beside her, fearful that she would be annoyed with him, and dared to reach out for her hand.

"Do you want to tell me about it?" he tried tentatively. She looked at him, the mask of cool resolve falling back into place despite the puffiness of her red face.

"It seems stupid now," she said, "like it doesn't matter anymore. That little boy in there has been through so much and he doesn't complain, doesn't fall apart…"

"Don't be silly," he told her gently, "some injuries never heal, not properly." She regarded him oddly then, trying to marry up the tough, bearded soldier with the kind and caring words of a therapist.

"Peter asked me about the scars," she said after a moment. Johnson nodded, looking at her intently as she spoke, as though he could lose her if his concentration wavered and the spell broke.

"I was married when I was eighteen," she began, "to a soldier. It was wonderful and new, but when I got pregnant my father insisted that we got married. We did, and as soon as we'd had a two-day honeymoon, he started hitting me." Her eyes locked with his, burning brightly with strength and pain in equal measures. "I lost the baby, which he blamed *me* for. My whole life was gone in an instant; I wasn't allowed out, I couldn't wear the clothes I wanted to wear, I had no friends…"

"Did he do that to you?" Johnson asked, his anger barely under control as he suspected the answer already, as his hand raised slightly towards the hair covering the puckered skin.

"Yes," she said, "he'd been court-martialled and discharged not long after we got married. He had a tendency to drink and get into fights. That made him worse. I'd burnt his food, according to him anyway, so he grabbed my hair and pushed my head down onto the hotplate. *'you don't listen'* he told me."

Johnson breathed in hard through his nose to try and tame the indignation and rage he was feeling at how this beautiful, strong and kind young woman had been so badly treated.

"So you went to the police?" he asked.

"Not directly," she said in a neutral tone, "but they were called. By the neighbours, I think. I stabbed him in his sleep a week afterwards, not that I remember doing it. He survived, unfortunately, and I spent four years in prison for it. Apparently, I was given a *lenient* sentence, on account of my temporary insanity. You know how many times I'd been to the local hospital in the year I lived with him?" she asked. Johnson opened and closed his mouth, unsure if the rhetoric needed a response.

"Thirteen," she told him flatly, "thirteen times in twelve

months with injuries I got from him. They asked me if I was sorry at the trial, they asked me to show *remorse*," her lip curled in disgust, "I told them I wished I had never met the bastard."

She stayed sitting there, staring off into painful memory for a while before she sniffed abruptly and stood up as though electrified.

"And there's me feeling sorry for myself, when a nine-year-old kid has survived this on his own literally, looking after a toddler. Put things into perspective, doesn't it?"

FIFTEEN

The two women and the girl tried to be as quiet as possible as they squeezed and pushed the mattress through the window of their room. When it was two thirds of the way out, hanging over the void, the lighter was clicked until the flame took hold. The foam scorched, melted, then caught in a sudden, toxic flash of flame which made them all choke and push at the burning lump with renewed energy to force it out of the window. Black smoke hung in the suddenly hot air of the small room as they all fought to crane their necks out of the opening at once to see where it landed. Their disappointment was palpable, as the burning mattress had landed fire side down and extinguished their attempts at arson.

"Grab more," Ellie said, "rip pieces off." They tore at the other mattresses, Jessica using the sharpened edge of her stolen teaspoon to slice at the stretched sections until they came apart in her hand. A kind of conveyor belt system established itself within seconds, with Jessica cutting pieces away using her adapted tool and Ellie passing them to Pauline, who set them on fire and dropped them one after another out of the window to the mattress below. They caught, spreading the fire until the darkness outside took on an eerie orange glow and an acrid smell sapped the oxygen from their immediate world.

"More," Pauline hissed, "keep it coming."

They did, and by the time shouts were reverberating loudly around the building, they had shut the window to their room, with only one mattress remaining. They had bundled up their few possessions and clothes into pillowcases and tied them together like bags, waiting for the commotion to build up. They put their coats on over their layers of clothing, holding their nerve collectively as they didn't want to be discovered.

Shout of 'fire' rang out loudly over the noise of doors opening and slamming and footsteps running fast down the corridors. They waited, breath held until some undetermined time when they should make a break for it. Their eyes met, darting between the three of them like electricity, until Ellie made the decision for them.

"Go!"

They went. Stepping fast along the corridor and down the stairs as doors opened and closed all around them. One man blocked their way, eyes wide and wild in the low light of the emergency bulbs, and he demanded to know what was happening.

"Fire!" Pauline yelled, repeating the panicked call that rang through the now busy building. The word was infectious some-how, spreading the disease of fear faster than the bites of the zombies ever could. People ran and jostled, pushed and shoved on the stairways to demonstrate their primeval terror of the untameable element. Nobody noticed their subtle luggage, nobody stopped them to question why they were fully dressed and wrapped up warmly against the cold night air when others were in disarray and clutching blankets around themselves. They continued the shout, using it as a catalyst for the panic and confusion that spread faster than the fire.

Outside, among the milling crowd of terrified people who

were foolishly all looking inwards when logic should have told them that the bigger threat came from the bright flames and the noise attracting attention from elsewhere, louder shouts of authority took command. One voice stood out above all of them, barking orders to some and instructing others to get out of the way. Water buckets were found but the frozen surface of the small pond there proved yet another barrier until someone who wasn't panicking found a large rock to drop in to break the icy surface.

As this activity churned, three figures slipped towards the back of the group, waiting again for the unfathomable right time to act. When the double echoing boom of consecutive shotgun blasts rang out from the approach road and the answering screams of fear rose and gathered momentum, the three figures knew that the time was right.

They didn't run, they simply faded away from the group and turned towards the darkness.

———

"What the hell is going on?" Michaels snapped at Nevin, who was still lacing his boots as he shouted orders.

"Fire," he said, "other side of the building on the outside. I'm having people put it out now."

"Fire?" Michaels asked incredulously, "How?"

"Haven't got that far yet, maybe we should put it out first so we don't burn the whole place down, and then we can figure that out afterwards?"

"It's a solid stone building, you moron," Michaels condescended nastily, "the worst that will happen is a few scorch marks if the fire is outside."

Nevin said nothing, only shot the man a murderous look that was mixed of embarrassment at not figuring that out and anger at being talked down to again.

"It's a diversion," Michaels told him after a moment of thought, "get every guard on the perimet…"

BOOM, BOOM.

The two men's eyes met in the poor light cast by the weak, yellowy bulbs. No words passed between them but instead a communication on a deep, almost telepathic level flashed as though they were speaking in the same high-frequency data-burst transmissions as the military radio sets. They ran towards the sound of the gunfire, Michaels pausing only to grab one of his armed men and order that every one of their guards be set to the perimeter immediately.

It was just one of them, passing by on their slow-motion travels in the freezing cold weather, and attracted by random chance to the noise and the smells and the bright orange flames licking up the side of the building. It turned towards the attractive sounds, its unthinking brain associating the disturbance with food, and it shambled uphill away from the road.

What remained of its nose was turned up into the air to sniff, and it detected the sweet scent of fresh flesh. Before the ravaged vocal chords could issue the high-pitched screech of attack, a bright blossom of flame and noise showed ahead. It rocked backwards, the torn rags of the shirt it had been wearing so many months before being blown away along with most of its right shoulder. The right arm hung limply, the muscles and tendons severed to make the two-handed reach only fifty percent effective. The second shot, the beautiful and deadly bloom of fire and lead erupting from the end of the shotgun's barrel took the entire left side of the face off the creature. As gruesome as the inflicted injures looked, they were far from effective at rendering the former person less danger-ous. The shocked and terrified guard fumbled with cold fingers inside thick gloves that denied him the sense of touch in locating a pair of fresh cartridges to charge the double-barrelled weapon again. He was forced to look down, to locate the new ammunition with eyesight in the poor light, and when he looked back up, he let out an animalistic squeal of pure horror.

With one useless arm hanging by gristly threads and half of what had once been a face scoured from the bone by the flensing shot, the thing bore down on him and drove him to the ground. He held the gun across his chest, screaming in short, pathetic gasps as he pushed the weapon out to keep the snapping jaws away from the exposed skin of his face. The rotting jaws opened and closed repeatedly, trying to find purchase and fulfil its sole purpose in life. It gave up trying to reach the face, instead turning and burying the broken pegs in its mouth into the thick sleeve of the waxed jacked the man wore. The bite force was unreal, sparking a howl of agony from the frozen sentry, but something inside him knew that the fight wasn't over; knew that the teeth hadn't broken his skin and told him that he still had a fighting chance to survive.

He abandoned the attempts to push it directly away from him, instead allowing the arm it was biting to drop and rolled it over away from him. He flew to his feet with a speed and flexibility he didn't know he possessed, struggling in a hideous tug of war which ended in the glittering of once-white teeth cascading through the air as the gripped sleeve was torn free. He staggered backwards a pace, righting his momentum, reversed the shotgun and brought the butt down savagely hard, twice, three times, until he stood and allowed the tears of fear and adrenaline to flow freely down his face.

He looked up at the sound of approaching footsteps; multiple and moving faster than any undead attack would have a right to. He smiled weakly at his reinforcements, grateful of the living company to tell his ordeal to, but blanched when he saw the face of the man who looked at him. Michaels regarded him coldly, eyes darting from the ruined head of the zombie to the man clutching at the arm which was already bruised by the sheer bite force of the attack. Something flashed between their eyes, another instant of communication, but this one was wrong.

"It didn't bi…" the guard managed, before Michaels raised the barrel of his gun and fired a bullet into his skull from three feet away.

Michaels and Nevin looked down on the two bodies lying at their feet, happy in their ignorance that they had contained any potential outbreak before it had started.

"Stay here," Michaels told Nevin, "I'll send someone to take over."

He walked away, thinking that he had a bad feeling something more sinister was happening.

———

"I'm stuck," hissed Ellie after she had helped Jessica over the barbed wire strands of a fence that had been recently repaired and reinforced. Pauline turned back, trying to help free the snagged denim on her thigh as the younger woman tried not to cry out from the stabbing pain.

"Hurry up," Jessica warned them, watching back up the hill in the direction they had slipped away from as louder shouts drifted down to them.

"Got it," Pauline told Ellie, shaking her hand to try and numb the pain of the metal stabbing into her thumb. Ellie's other leg went over the fence just as another hiss of warning came from the girl.

"They know," she said, her whisper an octave above where it had been previously, "they've got torches."

They did indeed have torches, and in the frost-covered grass of the slope leading away from the hilltop prison was a thick line of disturbed ground showing darker than its surroundings. The three women moved with renewed urgency as the threat of instant pursuit spurred them on. No more gunshots had come from the hill, but that didn't mean there wouldn't be any more if they were discovered.

"Which way?" Ellie asked as they reached a thick hedgerow at road level. Pauline didn't answer, she simply turned left and followed the line of the thick foliage for over a minute until she stopped and ushered them over a wooden style in a man-made break in the hedge. It was overgrown, but the gap was still big enough to let them through. They dropped down onto the roadway, the surface icy under the sharp crunch of old snow yet to thaw.

"Come on," Pauline hissed at them, taking off down the road at an uncertain pace due to the treacherous footing. They made as much ground as they could, slipping and helping one another when they lost their feet. Steam gathered around them in a haze as the moonlight illuminated them in a way that they couldn't see under the weak lights at the hilltop. Bathed in a shiny purple ethereal glow, they moved quickly, with their ragged breath coming in gasps. They knew they had to move fast, to put distance between those chasing them and themselves, but with each step the fear grew that they would be caught.

Jessica said nothing, but she was forced to stop when she was winded. She had no breath left and the painful stitch in her side doubled her over and made her recovery even less effective. Ellie noticed first, sensing that there was one set of footfalls too few, and turned back to her. Pauline hadn't noticed them stop, hadn't heard Ellie's hiss of warning, and with each second the gap between them grew wider. Ellie didn't dare shout, for there were still things out in the countryside that were more frightening than men with guns, but she was stuck between the two people she had fled with. She was closer to Jessica, and knew that Pauline would surely stop and wait for them when she realised she was alone. As Ellie walked to

Jessica, seeing the girl grimace and stand tall to try and catch her breath, she saw a curious haze of light behind her. It took her the half a dozen steps to reach her before her brain computed what the growing glow meant, and when she reached the girl she grabbed her and dropped to the ground, rolling them both into the ditch where the trickle of ice-cold muddy water threatened to take the breath away from them both. Jessica gasped, but the sound was barely audible over the grumble of an engine moving slowly along the road, following their obvious tracks.

The engine note waned, idled, then picked up again as the lights passed by Ellie and Jessica. Both of them squeezed their eyes shut tightly, hoping that if they couldn't see their pursuers, then perhaps their pursuers couldn't see them. Ellie realised as soon as the truck had passed and left them in darkness again that the tracks they'd left must have been confusing, but they hadn't stopped so instead the truck carried on.

Only one set of footprints left? Ellie thought. *What if one person was carrying the other?*

Quite why she reasoned the logic on behalf of the people hunting her she didn't know, but perhaps understanding your enemy was the key lesson.

"We need to go, now," she whispered in Jessica's ear. The girl's eyes shone brightly back at her as they reflected the power of the fat moon high above them. She nodded once, understanding what they now both knew.

They couldn't help Pauline.

They forced their way through the hedge to emerge in the field on the far side, then set off in a straight line across the dark countryside at an oblique angle to the road.

———

Pauline saw the road ahead of her grow lighter, just as the

unmistakable rattle of an engine reached her ears. She slowed, then stopped, and turned to face her impending humiliation and punishment as the truck lights illuminated her with full beams and made her turn her eyes away to save being blinded.

She had lost the other two somehow, but she had not seen or heard how or when they had disappeared. She knew it was some time ago, because all she could see as far as the distant lights were her own footprints; clear and very singular.

The truck stopped in front of her, the sounds of doors opening and closing, and a torch was shone directly into her face.

"How many others ran with you?" a voice demanded. Pauline said nothing, but smiled a sweet smile that had 'fuck you' emblazoned all over it. The man behind the torch hit her once, a brutally hard backhand that caught her between jawbone and cheek and sat her down with a sickening thump into the slushy snowmelt.

"How many?" the voice growled again, the promise of more pain evident in the tone.

"Five," Pauline lied with no idea why she said what she did, "three men and three women. We all split up."

Silence met her lies, underpinned by the chugging rattle of the truck engine.

"Bring her back," the voice said, "she can be an example."

As she was dragged to her feet and thrown into the hard back of the pickup truck, the man climbed in behind her and rested his cold, wet boot soles on her body.

"You cost us a guard," the voice of that bastard Nevin said, "and Michaels won't be pleased with you for that."

SIXTEEN

Dawn saw activity all over the region. The four-man SAS team deployed to seek more food and resources to both survive the winter and in preparation of making a very long and uncertain journey by road.

The three-person team slipped from their fortified village base with no fuss and even less noise, taking their van on a long-range scavenging run in the hopes of staving off starvation.

Nearer the coast, burnt wreckage and scorched mattresses were shoved over the cliff as the clean-up started at the hilltop. The rotten corpse of the lone attacker was discarded over the edge, along with the rest of the detritus but the dead sentry, dead at the hands of Michaels as everyone had heard, had apparently been popular. The others wanted a proper burial for him. They wanted to challenge the man over his account of their friend's death, as not one bite mark was evident on his body.

"You dig a bloody hole in frozen ground then," Michaels had spat at them, "because I wouldn't bother."

They did bother, despite how difficult and backbreaking it

was, and questions began to be asked about the woman who had been dragged back up the hill during the night. The people wanted to know what Michaels was going to do with her, and Michaels responded by telling the people that he would do whatever he damned well felt like doing, and if they didn't want to find themselves out on their ungrateful arses, then they would do well to stop questioning him. Those with questions faded away, and even some of those trusted with guns began to side with the majority.

Michaels, that evil bastard who was always beside him and who seemed to share the same mutual hatred for everyone and everything, and half a dozen others all clustered closely as though they could sense the change in mood.

The mood faded as most of those men left in vehicles to search for the missing men and women who had apparently fled in the night. Sneering down at the people who watched him leave, Michaels reached above him and pulled down the heavy hatch before the small tank he rode in drove away.

———

"Contact, north west," Mac called softly from his standing position with binoculars pressed to his eyes, "looks like multiple Screechers, standby…"

"Talk me in," Smiffy said, having abandoned his imitation of a television personality the instant Mac called the threat out.

"Past the stone cottage," Mac said, having widened his view to include the foreground briefly so that he could accurately describe the location to his sniper, "hedgerow following wes…"

"Got 'em," Smiffy cut him off, "just two by the look of it…" he went quiet as he watched the targets approaching them from a long way off. Downes and Dezzy were behind them somewhere, clearing out a larger building which would be useful for storing and sorting the supplies when they called the marines and the remainder of the squadron in.

"Don't seem that rotten," Smiffy said skeptically, "probably hibernated inside."

"Drop 'em," Mac instructed him, demonstrating his opposing ethos to their Major when it came to the undead. Downes was of the opinion that if they weren't close enough to threaten them, then it was a waste of a bullet, whereas Mac wanted to put down every one he ever saw, because it would need to be done eventually anyway and he wasn't one for putting off today's job until tomorrow. Smiffy took two longer, deeper breaths as Mac heard the click of the safety catch disengaging on the stolen Soviet rifle. He watched through the binoculars at the distant figures shambling over the field, waiting to see their fuzzy shapes drop in response to the sharp crack he expected to hear.

"Hold up," Smiffy said, "something ain't right with these…"

"What's not right?" Major Downes asked as he emerged silently behind them onto the low rooftop they occupied.

"Two dead bastards," Mac said, "coming in across country."

"Specify, what *ain't right*, trooper."

"Don't look that dead, Boss. Only… only sort of *half* dead," he replied, prompting silence as everyone brought out their optics to try and see what their shooter had seen.

"You know what, Smiffy?" Downes asked from behind his compact binoculars, "I think you might be right. Mac, Dez; left flank along hedgerow. Smiffy; with me."

———

Jessica didn't speak as she walked, just as Ellie behind her kept silent. Both of them were frozen to the core, filthy and soaked from the ditch water which hadn't dried from their clothes, despite having walked all night and through the dawn. Both were exhausted to the point of collapse, but neither wanted to stop as the fear of pursuit was constant in their minds. As they crested the rise and looked down into the shallow valley towards a small collection of houses and what looked like a village hall, Ellie simply pointed the direction they should head in and both trudged onwards, shivering in silence.

A crackle of twigs sounded ahead, making Jessica and Ellie snap their heads upwards to find themselves looking in the same direction. Both of them froze, and Ellie looked around on the ground for anything she could use as a weapon. Kicking at a lump of rock, she prised it from the stiff earth with difficulty. She hefted it in her right hand, pushing Jessica behind her, who clutched at the pathetically small sharpened teaspoon retrieved from her boot.

Nothing moved. No more sounds came from the thick hedgerow ahead of them, and their breath began to slowly return to normal.

"Put down your, er, *rock*, please," came a cultured and strong voice from over their left shoulders. Ellie yelped and spun, trying to push Jessica behind her again and only succeeding in tripping the girl, who fell to the frozen ground behind her and was too weak to get up. Jessica yelped then, seeing two men dressed in black clothing and carrying machine guns emerge from the bushes. Behind her, Ellie found herself looking into the clear, bluey-grey eyes of a tall man with his hands held out to show open palms. A gun hung on his chest, and various other dangerous looking items adorned his torso and waist, but his eyes pierced through everything to convey a message to the young woman that she was safe now.

Ellie dropped her rock, sinking to the hard earth beside Jessica, and both sobbed with exhaustion and relief.

———

Michaels had stopped talking to Nevin, solely because the man was annoying him. He wanted to go back, wanted to show strength in front of the others back at the Hilltop and maintain their control over the people. Michaels thought the man wanted to get back behind their defences and hide in the warmth, which was no bad thing in his opinion, but Michaels desperately wanted to find the people who had escaped his rule.

He had no idea it was just two women, or a woman and a girl, who were unaccounted for, but any loss was galling to him and he found himself pathologically unable to let it pass.

He had forced Nevin to stop their cramped armoured scout car, the Ferret with the thirty-calibre machine gun mounted on top and told the man to get out. The two of them walked carefully around a frozen, deserted village with their weapons held low but ready. Neither expected to be set up by any of the dead bastards out in the open, not in those temperatures, but it didn't pay to be complacent at any time.

That caution, that alertness, paid off when they both heard the sound of an engine at the same time. Their eyes met and, despite their almost obvious dislike for one another, both men recognised the need to work together. The Ferret was too far away, parked down a side street as it was too much of a giveaway to leave on the main road, and both men instinctively sought appropriate cover more attuned to the dangers of Northern Ireland than to a frozen southern English village amidst the undead apocalypse. The engine note grew, splitting into two distinct sounds with one lower, heavier note and another higher-pitched with a slight rattle. Michaels looked over at Nevin and caught his eye. He showed him a flat hand and waved it down in the cramped confines of the doorway he occupied. As awkward as it was, the signal for 'take cover' was obvious enough. Nevin nodded back, sinking out of sight into the shadows.

They waited for almost a minute before a dusty and frost-free box van rolled through the village. Michaels saw a flash of blonde hair, long and naturally straight, in the cab. Following after that, at a distance he could only describe as tactical, was a dirty beige Montego with a single male driver. Michaels waited until they had passed into silence, then rose to see Nevin emerging on the opposite side of the road.

"See the woman in the truck cab?" Nevin asked him. He nodded, having his guesses firmed up by Nevin's information.

"And what do you reckon was in the truck?"

"Well the signage said something catering, so…"

Michaels smiled, seeing that the two vehicles had left wide, black tracks in the freshly fallen dusting of snow that a blind child could follow.

"Come on," he said, "let's follow those tracks."

———

Downes and his men left Lieutenant Lloyd with the village they had cleared as they tried to keep the woman and the girl out of sight in the back of their adopted Land Cruiser. It wasn't that they didn't trust the marines, it was more that they saw no further need for excitement. They did consider requesting a loan of Marine Sealey, the only surviving medic from the island, but Smiffy said that he was capable of looking after them.

"It's just a bit of mild exposure," he said casually, "nothing a warm-up and hot drinks won't cure."

Water had been boiled on a small fire fuelled by solid white blocks that burned with a chemical intensity, and powdered hot chocolate was found in the hall. Dezzy found two mugs, added sugar liberally from the sachets he found in the kitchen area before pocketing as many as he could grab, and brought the drinks out to them, where they were safety wrapped up in blankets. Neither of them baulked or even pulled a face at the amount of sugar they were being force fed. Downes filled Lloyd in on their find, made their excuses and drove the frozen refugees back to the house. Neither spoke over the almost one hour they spent in transit, and both fell asleep leaning on one another, much to the annoyance of the two soldiers cramped in the boot space on top of their kit and radio. At least neither of them felt the urge to ask if they were nearly there yet.

Arriving back and threading the emplaced defences which visibly marred the approach to the attractive house, Downes looked back the way they had come. Fresh snow had fallen here when none had been seen in the valley they had searched, and their tyres made wide, dirty scrapes in the earth, which was adorned with vast coils of barbed wire strung between fenceposts driven into the ground at uneven angles between the neat excavations of earth from the trenches. In the frozen snow it looked just like the pictures he had seen painted from memory by the survivors of the Great War. The thought left him under a dark cloud, as already the death tolls of the two conflicts were horribly uneven.

"We're here," he announced, glancing at the woman and the girl, who had regained consciousness to blink and stare out of the windows. Neither of them answered him, not that he expected them to, given their recent ordeal, and they were ushered through the house to the warmest part, which had always been the kitchen.

"Sergeant Major Maxwell," Downes said comically, referring to Denise and not her husband through the intimate use of formality. The two had spoken at length on more than one occasion as they sat at the heavy butcher's block work surface. He found her to be every bit as reliable and essential to the effective running of the house as her husband was, having been thrown into the role of the senior NCO after the tragic loss of the Squadron Sergeant Major.

"Clive?" she answered quizzically, looking up from her task in the big, deep sink to stare at the bedraggled pair he guided into the room and steered towards the massive range, which radiated heat. "What's all this?"

"Found these two young ladies this morning, both rather wet and cold," he told her.

"Who are they?"

Downes hesitated a fraction longer than was normal, arousing suspicion in the woman. "They haven't spoken yet," he answered, worried that Denise would think he was palming off a problem onto her. She shot him another look, one that bordered on disappointment, and turned to the shivering arrivals.

"Hello, my loves," she said kindly, her eyes matching the smile and the warm tone of her voice, "what have you been up to then?" The question was rhetorical, as she fussed about them getting them seated beside the warm metal and pulling levers here and there before moving a metal pot onto a hot section of the old cooker to bring it back up to temperature.

That was the thing about the old kitchen, Downes thought to himself, it never got cold or switched off and was in a permanent state of tick-over until more was needed from it. It was like a living organism, more so than any modern, conventional kitchen would be.

"I shall leave you to it, Sar'nt Major," he said, ducking a small bow and retreating to shed himself of weapons and get into some drier clothing.

"I'm Denise," she told them as she wore the same wide smile, "we've been here a while now, and it's about half and half with us normal people and the army lot." She left out the variation of having RAF and Royal Marines there as it was only important to the people who lived by such acronyms and identities. If she hadn't been an army wife, then no doubt she wouldn't have cared either.

"What are your names?" she asked as she busied herself with the hot water and cups to make a drink.

"Ellie," the older one said. Denise couldn't place their relationship, as they could easily be sisters given the apparent age difference, but neither bore the slightest resemblance to the other physically. She knew that didn't mean anything as such, but she was a woman who trusted her hunches.

"And what about you, my sweet?" she asked, leaning down to put herself in the eye line of the younger girl.

"Jessica," she said, a hint of sullen anger in her voice, which was thick with cold and exhaustion.

"Well," Denise said as she looked up to meet the eyes of one of the other women who gravitated around the kitchens, "let's see if we can't find you some clean clothes to fit, eh?" she nodded to the newly arrived woman, one of her corporals she guessed, if the civilian mirroring of ranks and responsibilities was to be observed. The woman looked long and hard at the two people wrapped in blankets huddled by the warm hearth, nodded to herself and left the room clearly having taken all the measurements she needed.

"Who is in charge here?" Ellie asked through numb lips.

"Well," Denise said as she sat back on the wooden stool facing them and gently slapped her hands onto her thighs, "it was all a bit up in the air when we got here, but the Captain, that's Mr Palmer senior, is sort of in overall charge. There's Clive, Major Downes, who you know obviously, and Mr Lloyd has his marines. I run the kitchen, I suppose, and my husband is Mr Palmer's senior man. His little brother is here too, the other Mr Palmer, but he doesn't mix with us much..." She trailed off as she saw the perplexed looks from Ellie and Jessica.

"I'm waffling now," she said, "tell me how you ended up out in the cold?"

"We ran away from the place we were at," Ellie said, "and we… we…" she cast her eyes down as she couldn't finish the sentence.

"We lost the woman who came with us," Jessica finished with an edge of flint to her words, "they caught her. The men, not the others…"

Denise was shocked. Not being a woman usually lost for words she was speechless at the unspoken implications of what they had said.

"Were you… *prisoners?*" she asked finally.

"Yes," Ellie said, "and it was probably worse than you think."

———

They had been warmed, cleaned, dressed and fed before they were sat in front of a large fire crackling noisily in an ornate fireplace. There were four men in the room when Denise led Ellie and Jessica in. Downes they knew or at least had met already, and the others were introduced in turn.

"Ladies," said Denise Maxwell, "this is Captain Palmer." Palmer stood, offered a small bow and invited them to call him Julian if it pleased them.

"May I introduce Lieutenant Christopher Lloyd of the Royal Marines," he indicated a good looking young man with broad shoulders and a weathered face. "You have met Major Clive Downes of the Special Air Service," Downes smiled a greeting at them again, "and finally Mr Maxwell, our senior non-commissioned officer who reports directly to me and, of course, *Mrs* Maxwell, who *I* appear to report directly to some-times…" They all smiled at the weak but obvious joke and the newly arrived pair were invited to sit nearest the fire. As they did, a loud crack came from the flames and a smouldering ember spat out to land on the hearth.

"Our apologies for the poor firewood," Palmer said as though such things were under his direct control, "we have used up the stocks of seasoned wood and have been reduced to burning a coppice of ash we have found. It's quite green but won't suffocate us, I'm assured."

Ellie smiled to accept the unnecessary apology, feeling oddly at ease with the formality on display. He had a way, a manner, that made her feel far more elevated than her position had ever been.

"I understand," Palmer said gently, "that you have been residing at a place where the conditions were somewhat... *unpleasant.*" He left it as a statement. An invitation to explain and not a question that could be easily shut down with a simple yes or no.

Ellie told them. She told them everything from the moment she had fled with her daughter and hidden in villages as they went house to house for food to survive off. She told them about the men who had come and dragged her away, about the man in charge who had forced those same men to go back and look for her daughter, but who had come back with only news of her disappearance. She told them about the enforced work, about the women who kept the guards 'company' in return for items and certain freedoms. She told them about the rumours that the man in charge, this Michaels character, was forcing survivors to give him their food under the threat of violence against them. She told them about their plan to escape, about the pursuit and getting separated from Pauline, then walking all night and all day until they stumbled on the four soldiers.

"My sniper nearly shot you," Downes said, suddenly looking awkward as he tried to turn it around to show how much of an ordeal they had suffered as to look as though they were undead, rotting creatures.

"Hang on a minute," Maxwell said, glancing at his wife who had picked up on the same critical piece of information, "you said *Michaels*, right?"

"That's right," Ellie said, "they said he was a soldier too, just like the other one with the small tank."

"What other one?" Maxwell asked.

"Nevin," Jessica said, speaking for the first time during the meeting and curling her lip in hatred and disgust at the mere mention of the man's name.

Looks were exchanged through the room as almost everyone had some piece of information that others did not possess.

"Michaels was our missing troop sergeant," Maxwell said to the officers as an aside, "never showed up when the deployment call came in, so we chopped up his troop and shared the lads around others to fill the gaps.

"And Nevin?" Downes asked, having felt the overt hostility in the room at the mention of his name.

"Trooper Nevin," Palmer said with measured tones in a display of uncharacteristic anger, "was the bane of Mr Johnson's life. He is a lazy shirker, who is responsible for the bloodbath that led to the unfortunate..." he glanced at the young girl before choosing his next words carefully, "...passing of Sergeant Sinclair and his men. Trooper Povey attested to this, if you recall?"

They did recall. Not only was the loss of life a crippling blow to them as they had lost close friends and almost half of the remaining squadron strength, but the devastation that it was betrayal and cowardice of one of their own stung them deeply.

Palmer wanted to ask about Michaels, about his strengths and weaknesses as a man and a solider, but such conversations could be had with Maxwell in private.

"Ellie," Lloyd asked, "do you know where this Hilltop is?"

SEVENTEEN

Mike Xavier and Jean-Pierre burst back through the gates of the docks after yelling at his men guarding them to get the damned things open. They collapsed into a heap together, having run over half a mile through the thick fog and fearing that at any second they would have the undead fall upon them and tear them apart. Cans and packets of food littered the roadway as terrified men and women dropped their precious cargo in the fearful flight.

It was desperate, it was ill-disciplined, and it was a shambles. Xavier knew it as much as everyone else, and he felt responsible for it. He had been the one to yell at everyone to run when they had been attacked in the shop, and he knew in hindsight that he should have organised a dedicated guard and kept the others calm and orderly, instead of the mass panic they were now looking at with a destructive air of 'every man for themselves'.

He retained enough sense to order his men to take the food from the scavengers who flooded through the gate, each wearing similar looks of terror and relief in equal parts to be safely back inside the wire, but having seen the horrors that still existed out there. The pile of random foodstuff grew large. Large enough, he dared hope, to sustain them for a time. It would, if only he could ensure that some sort of order was maintained, because he had been horrified to see how rapidly normal people devolved to demonstrate the Darwinist theory of it being only the fittest who survived. He caught his breath, remembered what he must look like to the scared people who had been out there and deciding that he shouldn't be just as terrified as they were, and so he stood with his feet planted widely in the open gateway with the gore-smeared axe held in two hands.

"Put the food down there," he called to the people who trickled back in, opening his mouth to repeat the instruction to the shapes emerging from the fog but catching them in his throat as he began to speak them. The shapes morphed into two people, one of them being half carried with a limp arm slung over the neck and shoulders of another. Xavier froze, his heart rate feeling as though it had suddenly tripled, and the axe moved with a mind of its own as he let it swing low in one hand and draw back ready to take a batter's pose like he readied himself to play baseball.

"Stop there," he growled, "don't come any closer."

At the tone of his voice, instantly conveying fear and threat, Jean-Pierre appeared at his side, having abandoned his task of ensuring that people gave up their haul as they returned. Xavier felt the man's breath behind his neck, heard the miniscule gasp of air inwards as he saw what had prompted the challenge and recognised it immediately.

"She's okay," the person carrying the other shape called out weakly, "she just hurt her ankle is all."

"I said stop," Xavier warned again, real menace edging the words this time.

"No," pleaded the shape, coming into focus as the edges of the fog released them, "she's just twisted her ankle…"

At the mention of the afflicted area, Xavier and Jean-Pierre both glanced down to see the white ruffles of the woman's leg warmers soaked in a dark red. The blood had run through to her white trainers, showing a stark contrast with the other foot, and as their eyes glanced back upwards they saw her head lolling and her eyes rolling back into her head as though she was suffering from a fever. Her face was so white she seemed almost see-through. Her mouth moved constantly, weakly, as though she was trying to speak or suckle like a baby. Xavier knew he should say something, knew he should lay down the law and protect everyone and say something about the needs of the many outweighing the needs of the few or something like that, but the words just wouldn't come to him. His mouth flapped uselessly, just as the woman's did.

"You must leave her," Jean-Pierre snapped, "she has the sickness. She cannot come in here."

"But," the man protested pathetically, "please?"

"No," Xavier said, finally finding his voice, "she's infected and she will turn into one of them. She has to stay out there."

The look of ruined hope transformed in the man's eyes into a sudden and foul loathing.

"Who the fuck are you to say who comes in and who stays out?" his face contorted into a hateful rictus, and he saw the eyes of the two men barring his way turn suddenly wide and white in response. Filled with hope that he could intimidate them, he carried on.

"She's *fine*, now get out of my fucking way or else I swear to fucking *God*, I wi..."

The two men facing him flinched backwards as though he was about to vomit something noxious on them. He knew then that it was something else, something awful that had scared them and nothing to do with his anger. He had that sinking feeling that he was being watched, that something was behind him as the hairs on his neck stood up at oblique angles to his skin. Lowly, inexorably, he turned his head to look behind him.

He stopped when he had turned halfway to his right. He realised, too late, that the weight of the woman was no longer hanging on him and dragging him down. She was standing on her own, all reliance on him gone in an instant. Their eyes met, and despite the poor light and the heavy fog, the last thing he saw before the pain of teeth ripping the flesh from his neck forced his consciousness to flee was the milky white orbs or her eyes.

Jean-Pierre and Xavier moved as one. Like a choreo-graphed pair of dancers, they both moved forwards diagonally and crossed one another's paths to swing their weapons in almost perfect unison into the heads of the two unfortunate scavengers standing before them. As they dropped, screams sounded nearby as others witnessed the terror of the undead, stirred from their hibernation by the desperation of living humans for sustenance, reaching their gates.

As the captain and his first mate swung the gates closed just in time, two last healthy survivors ran in before the rotting smell hit them and the small wave of musty, hungry, zombies flowed out of the fog to reach for them.

The last man, clutching his shoulder, fell at Xavier's feet as Jean-Pierre locked off the gate and immediately reversed the heavy spike he carried to start puncturing skulls and crushing the cruel metal tip through eye sockets. The gate flexed worry-ingly, bending inwards under the weight of a concerted attack, the likes of which they hadn't suffered before as they had always kept a low profile. Xavier stood, grabbed a handful of the man's jacket and hauled him bodily to his feet with a strength that his thin frame didn't imply.

"Hey," he said to the man as he turned to leave. The nervous eyes rounded on his, almost pleadingly, until he saw

Xavier pointing to the bag of food he was carrying and directing him to leave it with the rest.

————

The panic subsided after an hour. The death toll was taken, and they believed that they had lost four from the names of people who were unaccounted for. Two of those were put down directly outside the gates and were visible, but the two others seemed not to have made it back at all. The food haul, however, was hardly worth it. They could expect to survive for maybe a week on what they had brought back, and that was only if it could be rationed out and protected. Without any real weapons there was no hope of maintaining order through force, and Xavier knew it was only a matter of time before they saw a repeat of the events which had led to their poorly planned shopping run.

He had recruited Jean-Pierre, who had agreed unques-tioningly as was his way with the captain he had known and sailed with for years, and two others. One was from his crew, a squat and unsmiling engineer known amongst the crew as Jase. Xavier didn't know if his real name was Jason or whether it was a nickname he didn't understand, but he filed that away with the whole raft of other shit he didn't need to know. He was completely taken aback by one of the other volunteers as one of 'the others' as he thought of them came up with the idea and wouldn't take no for an answer when she demanded to come with them. Philippa McAndrew was short and small, what some men would call petite but Jean-Pierre, who preferred his women big, said that she had the body of a young boy. That put Xavier off looking at her, given the unfortunate connotations of what JP had said, but there was no denying the fire in her. She had a broad accent, which to those who had never spent much time on the far side of the Atlantic would simply fall under the category of 'American'.

Her idea was for a small group, say no more than four, to take one of the many smaller boats from the dock to sail up or down from the city keeping close to land and hence staying well and truly off the radar of whatever warships patrolled the stretch of water between the mainland and Ireland. A small group would also allow them to keep a low profile and not attract any of the things out there, and that way they could bring back food without causing a big commotion like they had earlier.

Xavier tried to let the implied criticisms ride, but her words put him in a dark mood.

"I don't know how you do things in America," he said, "but over here it's not polite t…"

"Canada," she said flatly, cutting him off.

"Eh?"

"I'm from Canada, not America, but please, you were saying?"

Xavier felt all fight evaporate from him in annoyance as he realised he had nothing to say in the first place. He diverted the conversation with practicalities.

"You got a weapon?" he asked her.

"I'll find something," she said, "when do we go?"

Xavier looked at Jean-Pierre.

"As soon as you've got a weapon," he told her.

———

The small white fishing boat chugged lazily out of the docks and turned south to skim along the dark waters of the River Mersey in search of food.

Back at the port, in the bowels of *The Maggie*, where the survivors all huddled for warmth and companionship to stave off the fear and the cold, one man was absent from the group. He had taken himself away, as the noises he was making were threatening to draw attention to him He gasped and moaned as he burned up from the inside with a fever the likes of which he had never known or even thought possible. He rocked in the corner of the bathroom, hidden behind the dirty shower curtain as if believing the filthy plastic sheet could block out the world and keep him from being discovered. The only lighting there came from the weak glow of an emergency bulb, but with eyes accustomed to the dark it was enough to see in at least some detail. Slowly, stifling the sobs as he inched the material up his arm, he exposed the bite mark on his wrist. It was swollen, angry, and in place of what he would expect to be red flesh there was black. Or at least such a dark purple that it seemed black in the low light. He knew he had been infected, but the fear of receiving an axe to the head was somehow more terrifying to him than dying a slow and painful death through the fever which tortured his body. He was too frightened, too fevered, to know what would happen when he finally succumbed to the sickness, and he couldn't help himself. He closed his eyes, resting the burning skin of his face against the cool tiles of the shower cubicle, and he fell asleep.

He awoke sometime in the dead of the night, in as much as his body began to move when what had made him *him* had fled; chased away by the temperature soaring in his brain and killing off every conscious part of the man who had once inhabited the body. He stood, seemingly full of power and rage as pain and hunger no longer affected him as it once had. He staggered from the shower cubicle as the plastic sheet slithered over his face until gravity pulled it down behind him, then his head snapped to the right in response to a sound; a single cough, low and soft, but the unmistakable sound of something living nearby. He sniffed the air, an animalistic and predatory gesture which sparked him onwards towards the narrow cots set up all along the section of the large ship. He found the first beating heart, the first hot skin to meet his teeth, sleeping in an alcove near the toilet block. Only a choking, gurgling sound came from the person as they gasped without vocal cords or the supply of blood to the brain. The hot, sticky fluid fountained upwards so hard that the flow atomised on the metal roof above their makeshift bed and sent a fine red mist to drift down over them. The first man chewed on the mouthful of crunchy sinew and stringy meat for a while, until something made it stop and regard its victim. The milky, blind eyes found themselves mirrored by a similar stare, and slowly the first man opened his mouth to allow the chewed flesh and pipes to drop out of his foul maw. The second man rose, walking off in a direction for no known reason and not bothering to check if the first man had followed him. He had in fact followed, solely because the movement and noise attracted it to the behaviour of its victim, which now somehow led the way for him. They killed as a pair, chewing great lumps from men and women indiscriminately until a horrified scream sounded the alarm. By the time they had been discovered there were five of them animated, all following the second one of them to have been turned, and as the main sleeping area awoke to the terror of shouts and screams, they all tried at once to get through the single door leading away from the threat.

New sounds answered those screams, as the unholy shrieks of all but one of the newly turned beasts sounded horribly loud in the metal confines of the ship's belly. What followed was a bloodbath, where the only escape to be had was either over the side of the ship into the icy blackness below, or else out of the docks and into the foggy city where death would just take a little longer to find them.

EIGHTEEN

Nevin drove slowly, keeping the revs of the Ferret low and thereby reducing the chances of them being detected. They didn't need to maintain visual contact with them, as the tracks they left in the snow were like a shining beacon that just cried out to be followed. Those tracks eventually stopped at a barricade in a country road between two large properties on the edge of a small village. They left their vehicle far away from the village and went back on foot, both carrying their weapons, to spy on the barricade.

Voices reached them, drifting back on the wind, and not raised carelessly as they would be if amateurs resided there. The height of the barricade meant that they could see nothing, and Nevin turned to Michaels and indicated with hand signals that he was going to skirt around the village. He added a gesture to tell Michaels to stay where he was, but the raised eyebrow made it clear he had overstepped the mark. Nevin said nothing more, only went and wished that he could take the keys to his Ferret, when like all military vehicles, the damned thing started on a switch and couldn't be overridden.

He went slowly, hugging the ground low and keeping his

eyes and ears alive to the risk of discovery. He went to the left, to the lower ground, and tracked a small brook which bubbled and raged in its own tiny way, with the additional water flowing in between the rocks and chunks of ice. He stopped, finding the smallest of gaps to peer through in the prickly hedge running beside the stream, when he saw something that he didn't expect; that was, if the people inside had been tactically minded. In the gloomy air outside, the shining beacon of artificial light coming from the wide windows and double doors of the kitchen shone like a beacon, even though the sun had yet to start its decline with any purpose.

The light didn't surprise him, but what did take his breath away and threaten to rob him of all stealth and sense was the shape he saw in the kitchen.

It, *he*, was unmistakable. The size of him. The sheer presence, despite having clearly lived in the wild for weeks or more, given the beard he now sported. The cut of his large shoulders and the disapproving, threatening cut of his brow.

Johnson. Squadron Sergeant Major Dean Fucking Johnson.

The man had terrorised him. Hit him, on more than one occasion, and never missed an opportunity to humiliate or punish him. He was the reason that Nevin had escaped the bounds of the army, had abandoned his mates – or at least the men who should have considered him as a mate – to death and fear when he had ensured his own safety.

If he's here, Nevin thought to himself, *then where is the rest of the squadron?*

His logical mind told him that half, or maybe a third, of the squadron was destroyed when he had got clean away, but then he recalled that *Mister* Johnson had never made it back. He had been stranded on the island or, if the helicopter had even made it there to lift them out, he was lost somewhere, along with a load of the marines.

Nevin settled in to watch. He saw the owner of the blonde hair they had both seen in the truck cab, and he smiled evilly at her uncommon looks. She was no beauty, not in his opinion anyway, but she had a look that was *different*. He saw another woman, one that he had recognised from the island, as well as the short sergeant of marines and another bearded man he didn't recognise.

That's four, Nevin thought, *and none of them is from the squadron.*

He assured himself that Johnson was stranded, cut off from the main group, if they even still lived, and had met up with others. They must have fortified their little village and thought themselves safe, but he guessed that they hadn't counted on having to defend themselves against an enemy with heavy machine guns. He slithered back to Michaels, finding him gone from where he had left him, and so he jogged back awkwardly on the frozen ground to find him lounging on the angled hull of the Ferret with a cigarette hanging from his mouth, as he had his hands stuffed deep in his pockets and his collar turned up against the icy breeze.

"Well?" he asked.

"You wouldn't fucking believe it," Nevin answered in an excited whisper, "It's bloody Johnson!"

"Who?"

"Johnson!"

"Hang on," Michaels said as the penny dropped, "*Johnson,* Johnson? The SSM?"

"Yeah, and it looks like there's only a few of them there with all the food in that truck they found."

Evil mirrored evil as their eyes met, both of them feeling an air of excitement at taking from others, especially others who had ruled their lives with strict discipline.

"How many is a few?" he asked.

———

"Shh," Astrid Larsen said abruptly as she held up a finger, "did you hear that? The engine sounds?"

"I heard nothing," Enfield said. From anyone else the speed of his answer might have sounded dismissive, but she knew him well enough to know that he was always tuned in to his senses. She relaxed, satisfied that she had imagined the sound of revs picking up before dropping into a higher gear.

They carried on unloading the truck, carrying large sacks of dried pasta, wearing smiles that only the promise of a full belly could warrant. There was rice and flour too, as well as huge catering tins of baked beans and mushy peas. It wasn't going to be winning any awards for style and presentation, but their dinner would be packed full of much needed calories.

They ate together, the mood high despite the bitterly low temperatures outside, and for the first time in as long as they could remember, they were full. It didn't go to waste, as the leftovers were sealed in Tupperware tubs and placed outside on the patio. One plate with half a portion left untouched wasn't saved, however, as the scraggy cat had leapt silently onto the worksurface to lap at the sauce until it was noticed. It froze, growling in a way that was almost funny, and shook its head rapidly to kill the pasta shell it held between its teeth.

They went to bed, with no idea that their safe haven was firmly in the crosshairs of men who had learned to enjoy the pain of others.

———

The mood at the Hilltop was sullen, awkward even, and both Michaels and Nevin received curious looks when they returned.

"What the fuck is that all about?" Nevin moaned to

Michaels, who simply huffed in response to simultaneously indicate that he neither knew nor cared. Orders were given, men and women were armed, and a scrawny goat was taken from the shed it lived in to be dragged reluctantly to the back of a truck by the rope around its neck.

The fighting men, and a couple of women in the same bracket, left the Hilltop without reassurance or communication with anyone there. A handful of guards, now more worried about their leadership than either the zombies or the men and women under their 'protection', shot nervous and sullen looks as they were left alone and outnumbered by the small population who seemed ready to revolt. One guard in particular was wary, the one keeping the door firmly shut on the woman who was locked inside after her attempt at escape. The guard was finding that her evident popularity with the crowd was in directly inverse proportions to his own. The small crowd gathered, saying and doing nothing except watching him and the door he was blocking. He was so intimidated by the passive aggression of these unmoving people that he wanted back-up and demanded that other guards join him there. Barring the way with their shotguns, almost half of the armed guards left behind ended up huddled in that doorway before long. If any more were required there, it would seriously hamper the security of the main approach as they were already spread thinly enough.

If Michaels and Nevin didn't get back soon, they thought, then they wouldn't be coming back to the same place they left.

The uprising was ready to start; all it needed was a spark.

———

The three vehicles – an estate car, a farm pickup and a Ferret scout car with a turret-mounted thirty-calibre heavy machine gun – chugged at a gentle pace through the countryside. They went via a very circuitous route, stopping at every village and town to kick in doors where they could and make enough noise to invite anything preserved inside to shuffle forth into the harsh glare of a snow-covered landscape. The hibernating zombies woke. Whole families, as they once had been, staggered outside on stiff limbs in response to the sounds and smells of fresh, living meat. Each settlement they passed through prompted more followers, and the desperate bleating of the tethered goat attracted them inexorably onwards as the convoy pressed on. They had established a pattern; accelerating as they approached a village, dismount, kick doors in or open them, return to the vehicles and make noise until the leading edge of the herd following them caught up. Rinse and repeat.

There weren't many dead preserved inside, and some villages held none at all, but they had amassed enough of an undead infantry division that by the time the Ferret pulled ahead to lead the way to the fortified settlement they wanted to attack, there were close to fifty zombies, all dry and musty in various shapes and sizes and states of undress following in their wake.

The goat was never going to be a winner in this scenario, and when the three vehicles pulled off the main road ahead of the small herd and the goat was dragged, pulling and bleating loudly, from the pickup they could see the approaching micro-horde speed up as the smell and sound of the distressed animal reached their senses.

Nevin didn't so much volunteer for the job, but he didn't really object either. To be the one who acted so bravely to take down Mister Bloody Johnson was an accolade he would be happy to live with, after they had broken down their defences and taken what they had.

He moved slowly, angry at the incredible strength the wiry goat had summoned up, but when it smelled the rotten flesh behind it, there seemed to be no more argument about which direction they should head in. Nevin stooped, scooped the animal up bodily despite the struggling, and dumped it over the vehicle barricade with difficulty. He heard a crunch as the animal landed, unseen on the far side, and instantly the bleating ramped up in volume, intensity and frequency. The thing positively screamed, and Nevin smiled sickeningly as he guessed it must have broken something as it fell to the frozen roadway on the other side.

Happy with the results, he ducked away to double back to the safety of his armoured vehicle as the zombies shrieked and moaned to fight one another and jostle for the lead position as they zeroed in on the injured goat.

Game on, he thought to himself.

———

The sound of a baby crying made them all freeze. Wide eyes met others that mirrored their shock and disbelief, and as one they all scrambled for their coats and weapons to pour outside. The sight of a goat, one front leg held off the ground and dangling as the thing bleated constantly in high-pitched protestation at the pain, confused them all.

"What the…" Hampton began, just as Enfield pushed past him and raised the small rifle to drill a bullet into the goat's eye socket.

"…hell?" he finished.

"Noise like that will attract everything for miles," Enfield said, "like a bleeding fish flapping in the water, the sharks'll come."

The now dead goat still held everyone's attention, as the blood poured out in pulsating gouts to soak the snow red. When the sound of the injured animal had echoed away to nothing, another sound, one far more ominous and recognisable, filled the air like a hum.

Shrieks, far off but still too close, and the moaning, wheezing sounds of air being driven in and out of lungs which no longer seemed to need it appeared to surround them.

"Bags," Johnson hissed, "everyone in the catering truck just in case, *now!*"

By everyone, he meant Kimberley and the children, as the others were already launching into action. Enfield threw himself up a ladder lashed to the side of a house with a small balcony that offered a commanding view of the road. He hefted the small civilian rifle he had grown so fond of, but still had his beloved Accuracy International sniper rifle on his back, despite the limited number of bullets he had left for it.

Peter had gone back inside for Amber, smiled at her and helped her sweep up the stuffed lamb and toys into her bag before hurrying her down the stairs to slip her little feet into her Wellington boots and wrap the new padded wax jacket around her. He added a scarf and a hat until only her eyes were visible, then bundled her and the bags he carried into the truck.

She didn't fall for the false smile and the higher-pitched voice offering her reassurance that everything was alright. She wasn't stupid. She knew something was very, very wrong. She didn't even flinch when the sharp snapping cracks of Enfield's measured shots pierced the air. Peter left her there, returning shortly afterwards wearing more layers and throwing bag after bag into the back of the truck and holding his trusted spike aloft before smiling at her again and disappearing from view. Other sounds rang out, confusing her with what sounded like stones being thrown hard against metal in closely-grouped twos and threes. Amber sighed, pulling the dirty stuffed lamb from her bag and nudging down her scarf, she pressed the worn material to her lips and waited for it to end.

"Where did this lot come from?" Hampton asked, his own rifle still unfired as he among all of them carried an unsuppressed weapon. The increase in the intensity of the attack made him rectify that as the louder noise of his weapon joined the fray.

"Fuck knows," Bufford answered, his voice distorted by his right cheek being pressed hard into the stock of his weapon as he moved and fired, moved and fired, picking off the skulls of the nearest Screechers to prevent them from reaching the barricade.

A shriek tore the air behind them as a cluster of three or four emaciated monsters had worked their way inside through a weakness they hadn't known existed. They were at the rear of the truck, reaching inside and snapping their blackened teeth at the warm flesh of the precious cargo. Johnson heard the shriek of the Screechers in attack, turning and raising his weapon just as a hatchet blade swept downwards into one skull, and a two-pronged spike burst from the back of the head of another. Three more attacked over their dying comrades, unthinking and uncaring as to their fate, and as Johnson lined up to riddle their brains with bullets, the huge booming report of a shotgun firing filled the air. One of the heads he was aiming at fell away, half severed by the scattering lead storm, then another popped open like a hard-boiled egg. Johnson bit down his revulsion and drilled a pair of bullets into the remaining zombie. He ran forward, kicking the bodies clear of the open tail section, and glanced inside to see Peter concentrating, with his tongue sticking out the side of his mouth as he forced his shaking fingers to slot new cartridges into the sawn-off shotgun. He locked eyes with Kimberley, her own weapon dripping gore, and he jumped to drag down the roller shutter lower in readiness to leave. They were fighting all around now, and the end was inevitable.

Johnson, unfamiliar MP5 squeezed tightly into his shoulder,

pinged off rounds in ones and twos, depending on how accurate his opening shot had been. He held his head up away from the weapon to view the bigger picture, and he saw it at the same time as Bufford and Astrid. None of them had chance to call it before their sniper shouted down the warning to them from his perch.

"Too many," he called out, "fall back."

It was the worst news they could receive, and it spelled dread for them. They knew they could never have stood a chance against the kind of hordes they had experienced back when it began, but those mass gatherings, those unexplained events, those undead singularities had all but stopped as soon as the weather had begun to turn towards winter. They had dared to hope that they wouldn't be forced to face down another crowd, but none of them was so naïve as to think that they couldn't one day be surprised by the Screechers. That was why their immediate plan was to bug out, to withdraw, in the opposite direction of the attack if they ever found themselves facing an onslaught like they did now.

Despite planning for it, expecting it even, the savagery and speed of the wave of dead meat emerging from the countryside took their breath away with how fast things could go from normal to neck deep in shit.

"Pull back," Johnson echoed, hearing a rising flurry of muted gunshots as the defenders on the line upped their intensity at the risk of reduced accuracy. It was a vestige of training against an enemy that had a fear of incoming bullets. It was designed to make any attackers put their head down to avoid the incoming rounds and give those defenders precious moments to move. Bufford and Astrid reloaded as they ran, their movements instinctive and well-practised, and they climbed aboard one by one as Johnson started the truck. Hampton paused at the back, looking up at the only man of his unit left alive as far as he knew. Enfield wasn't shimmying down the ladder to join him. He wasn't even looking in the direction of the attacking wave of zombies, but instead he was staring aghast behind him and rapidly struggling to slip the strap of his larger rifle free of his shoulder to bring it to bear on the road leading away behind them.

Hampton followed his gaze, looking up at the small rise in the road behind them questioningly with his breath held. He expected to see the heads of yet more zombies appearing at any point; expected a larger horde to attack them from the rear, but instead he saw the dull green painted metal of a British army military vehicle. His heart soared for the briefest of moments, suddenly happy that the others had found them and rescued them at the best possible moment. He turned to shout to the others that the squadron was there, that they could help them take on the horde, but just as he did the impossibly loud clattering sound of a heavy machine gun erupted from behind him. He followed the flashes of tracer ammunition, which over the short distance it fired made it appear as though laser beams were being shot from the turret of the small tank, and those beams aimed directly up at the small balcony of the house where Enfield had been.

"Go!" Hampton roared as he hopped down painfully, pulling closed the roller shutter of the rear of the truck as he did, pushing Astrid bodily back inside as she had moved to follow him, before slapping a flat hand twice on the side of the vehicle, "get out of here!"

In the front seat beside Johnson, Bufford looked wide eyed at the SSM and shook his head. The message was clear; no way could they get out if they stayed to mix it with whatever living enemy now attacked them.

One word ran through Johnson's mind: Nevin.

It could only be him, much the same as the vehicle being used to assault them was the same Ferret they had heard in the town where Enfield had been fired upon. They were stuck.

Stuck like rats in a barrel and the lid was closing fast. They had only one option to get away, and that was to force open the barricade in front of them against the tide of Screechers and drive away, leaving their two marines to an unknown fate.

"Fucking *go!*" Hampton yelled again, barely audible over the big gun firing on full automatic and disintegrating the house as great chunks of tiled roof and masonry fell away.

"We can't leave them," Johnson said, knowing it was foolish to hesitate or even consider staying to fight alongside them against far superior forces, even if the undead weren't attacking them at the same time.

"We have to," Bufford told him. "You'd do the same."

He knew he would. He would sacrifice himself to give the others a chance at escape, a chance to get the kids out to safety no matter how slim their odds of survival. Johnson closed his eyes momentarily, glanced in the driver's side mirror at the small but devastatingly impervious vehicle behind them, and he let up the clutch to jolt the truck forwards. It bumped into the barricade, into the part left on reasonably preserved rubber instead of flat metal, and he used the torque of the diesel engine to force it clear. Screechers fell under the weight of the rusting, cold metal and the way the car swung outwards cleared a path for their truck to nose its way out of the village and leave behind not only their friends, but all of the hard work and hope and stored supplies they'd been relying on.

NINETEEN

Enfield saw the turret swing towards him and, for the second time in this short episode in his life, he found himself the unfortunate focus of attention for the commander and gunner of the Ferret and the current subject of the thirty-cal machine gun's attention. He hadn't had a chance to even bring the Accuracy International up to his eye before the huge bullets tore the air towards him. He threw himself backwards, straight through the single pane window of the house with the pretty balcony set at the perfect height to look out over the fields as though there was no village there.

The concussive ripping booms of the big projectiles hammering past him was deafening, and he could think of nothing other than trying to get clear of the onslaught. He lay on the musty carpet of the bedroom, glass and brick dust falling over him as he closed his mouth and forced his eyes shut. He crawled forwards blindly, trying to put any distance between him and the gun even if it was a few pathetically desperate feet of bedroom floor. He opened his mouth, gasping a breath in and immediately choking it out as the dust stuck to his throat. He coughed it out, sensing a break in the firing by the absence of the waves of pressure as opposed to the lack of noise. As his hearing returned to him, a more familiar sound reached up to his hiding place; the crackle of an SA80 rifle firing bursts of automatic 5.56. Enfield furrowed his dust-covered brow in thought.

Why would Bill Hampton be firing small arms at a bloody tank? Surely he wouldn't waste the ammo.

Another noise pierced his consciousness, this one dialling into his sense to inspire fear at a molecular level. The shriek of the Screechers sensing fresh meat fired a round straight to his fear receptors as it sparked something so primal in him. His fuddled and assaulted brain made the tenuous connections between the gunfire belonging to his sergeant and the attention of the undead bastards drawn to the noise, and all thoughts of the scout car and its evil thirty-cal were forgotten as he forced himself back to his feet to return to the ravaged remains of the once picturesque balcony.

Only part of the standing area survived, and great chunks of the exterior wall of the house had disappeared. Piles of rubble rested on the frozen ground below, and Enfield regained the cold, clear air of the outside world in time to see the back tyre of the Ferret bounce over a lump of stone with a swathe of off-yellow cladding still attached to it. The cladding crumbled away under the weight of the heavy wheel, but the attention of the gunner had passed him by. The turret swung to the left, the barrel depressed and a long, rippling burst of fire spewed from it as it rolled forwards. The sound of Hampton's rifle went quiet, stopping at the same time as a yelp of pain and the crumbling rumble of a collapsing building. The Ferret went on, switching its aim to point dead ahead where it fired burst after burst of rounds dead ahead, no doubt to try and bring down the escaping box truck which symbolised the entire reason that he and Hampton had stayed behind in sacrifice; so that they could get away.

He saw sparks ping off the left side of the scout car as it was stopped, paused in the gap in the barricade as the driver shunted it back and forth to get the correct angle to escape the village enclave. The car stopped as the turret swung to the left in search of a target. Elated that Hampton was still alive enough to shoot at them, Enfield's sudden happiness was marred with the knowledge that his sergeant was about to be riddled with heavy calibre bullets.

He blinked his eyes to clear the dust from his vision, shook his head to reset his senses, and pulled the heavy rifle into his shoulder to take aim at the single point of vulnerability for small arms. It was a difficult shot; difficult to the point of impossibility but he wasn't just anyone with a gun.

He was an expert. He was the consummate professional, and his chosen profession was accuracy. He could put a bullet wherever he wanted, and right then he aimed for the tiny slats of the left side viewing port where the gunner would be looking out of.

It was desperate, but it was all he could do. He aimed, not having to correct for wind of drop of the bullet but putting the crosshair above his target as he was firing at a tenth of the range that the big rifle was sighted for, and he fired.

———

"Who the fuck is doing that?" Michaels asked over the headset, not expecting Nevin to answer.

"Doing what?"

"Some twat's shooting at us! Left side. Stop a minute…"

Nevin chuckled nastily and stopped the Ferret as he kept his eyes forward in search of the truck that had disappeared. Most of the zombies they had herded were dead now; crushed by wheels or else thrown down by bullets. They had driven around to the far side of the village to barge their way through the barricade as soon as the attack came from the other side. Nevin was impatient, he wanted to press ahead and chase down the box truck to take whatever was in the back of it. The six others hiding in their cars nearby, ready to move in and take the stockpiles, would stay hunkered down until they had rolled through and dealt with every threat. As much as he wanted to chase down Johnson, who he had guessed was in the truck, he did as he was told and waited for Michaels behind him to spin the barrel of the gun and deal with the idiot who might as well have been throwing rocks at them. The man behind him manning the gun was consumed with a swift victory, distracted by the destruction of their undead conscripts, and he had broken his own cardinal rule.

Never leave an enemy in your rear. Ever.

Nevin waited, looking forwards until a hollow, metallic scream echoed inside the cramped interior and deafened him with a ringing thrum. He couldn't understand what had happened, and in his deafness, he tried to speak and heard only a muted croak in his head; as though he could feel the vibration but not hear the sound. He dabbed his fingers at his head, feeling hot liquid on his skin and looking down in disbelief at the bright blood. He reached back to his scalp, feeling sharper chunks alongside the hot gelatinous globules adorning his hair, and he squirmed in his seat to view the gruesome destruction wrought by a single armour-piercing bullet aimed at precisely the right spot.

It had been Enfield's second bullet that had managed to penetrate the latticed metal of the viewing port. Michaels leaned towards the aperture, pressing his face right up to the gap just as the bullet pierced the armoured skin and twisted to warp and break apart. As it did, the trajectory of the spinning lump of metal varied to pass through the bridge of his nose and blew his right eye out through the temple. He was dead before he knew that he had even been shot, before he could sight in on the injured man in camouflage combat uniform and finish him off, and his lifeless body slumped behind his driver with half of his face blown away. The bullet embedded itself inside the cramped interior somewhere, missing the driver by mere inches as he had no idea what had happened.

———

Enfield let out his breath, taking his eye away from the scope slightly as his hand moved the well-oiled bolt and his fingertips caught the expended bullet casing as he had with every carefully placed round he had ever fired through the weapon. The turret stopped moving and the Ferret stayed still for a long time. The sniper was weakened by his desperate escape from the gun, and he wavered and lowered the gun as his legs threatened to give out. He slumped down, the pain across the back of his right shoulder erupting in an agony he had never thought possible, and he slid off the destroyed edge of the balcony to land heavily on the cold ground below. He blinked slowly, each closure of his eyes getting longer than the last, until the darkness and the cold took over.

———

Nevin, when his senses were restored, had to stifle a laugh. He weighed up the pros and cons: It was unfortunate that Johnson and the others with him had escaped, and it was less than ideal that whatever guns and food they had stockpiled were mostly gone with them. There were stacks of shotguns and plenty of ammunition for them, but the obvious lack of anything good combined with the missing people made it clear that they had missed out on something.

It was good, despite the shock and the gore adorning the back of his head, that Michaels was gone, because it left it wide open for him to take over the Hilltop as his own. It was far easier to return with his body from what he could call a successful raid, abandon Michaels' despotic vision of hunting escapees down and generally make life feel a little easier for everyone who would be happier to serve him and make his life rosy.

The vile winter would end eventually, and after that he would enjoy himself. He had even decided to be generous, ordering the shocked foot soldiers he had travelled with to take everything from the big house and help him drag the near-headless body out of his wagon. One of them asked if they should bury Michaels.

"Would he waste time and effort digging a hole for you?" Nevin asked them in return. No threat or malice in his voice, only the stark honesty of his words which resonated with the others. They took what they wanted from the village, dispatching the few lurching, staggering corpses that remained in the area. A few stragglers had followed the main group but moved more slowly than the others, and they had to be dealt with by the two people left on guard. Nevin stayed in the Ferret, electing not to add a gunner to sit behind him as it would take too long to train someone in the very basics of how the gun operated. He decided to recruit a driver for himself at some point in the near future, but his list of considerations was huge and growing by the minute. He saddled up his small force, looking back at the destruction they had wrought on their unsuspecting enemy with a cruel satisfaction.

———

After they had left, when silence had descended on the once peaceful village, along with the soft blanket of fresh snow, a pile of bricks thrown down from the corner of a partly destroyed house shifted to cascade rubble and the powdery white dust to the dark smears exposed by the movement. Sitting up and looking around with a stunned sense of confusion, Bill Hampton tried to figure out what had happened. The last thing he knew was that he'd been firing a pointless barrage at the armoured vehicle in impotent rage, just as a final 'fuck you' to try and spend his life giving the others an extra second to get away. The turret had spat flame in his direction, deafening him as heavy bullet after heavy bullet tore down a section of wall behind. Massive chunks of masonry and brickwork had fallen on him, striking him hard in the back of the skull and burying him under the rubble. Now, awake and only half sensible, he clawed his way out of the pile of bricks and dragged himself along with no idea where he was heading. He made it to his feet uncertainly, staggering like one of the undead, only less aware of the world surrounding him.

He found a piece of metal in a pile of rubble that didn't belong, a straight line protruding up at a diagonal angle, and he dropped to his knees to follow the cold pipe into a small snowdrift to trace its origin. It wasn't a snowdrift, but merely a barely warm body covered in camouflage material, blood, brick dust and fresh snowfall.

"Get up," he grumbled thickly through a mouth full of dust and blood, "on your fucking feet, lad."

The pile groaned, moving to expose a vicious red line scored across the burnt patch of uniform. Hampton pulled at him, dragging him out and falling backwards off his knees for them both to land nearly face to face. The battered features of marine sniper Enfield came slowly into focus and opened his eyes to regard his sergeant.

"Sarge?" he croaked, like a child emerging from a nightmare and seeking the comfort of a parent.

"It's me, lad," he said kindly, "it's me. I've got you."

Enfield came around as slowly as Hampton had, and broke out into a crippling shiver, whereas the older man seemed not to feel the cold. He looked at the thing in his hands, the beautifully crafted weapon capable of killing at over a mile away if the person holding it had the requisite skill. Enfield had the skill, but he no longer had the weapon. Somehow, probably during the fall he knew he must have had, the breech of the gun had struck a rock hard and bent out of shape. Even if it could be mended to allow the trapped bolt to run smoothly free, he wouldn't trust it not to explode with the first bullet he would fire through it. His beloved gun was gone; sacrificed to the fight and having earned its place by that sacrifice. Enfield looked around dumbly, not sure what he needed, but totally sure that he needed something. He felt naked somehow, and incomplete.

Unaware of his desperate confusion, Hampton's eye landed on a dark colour among the snow-covered detritus. He stumbled to it, dragged it free of the fallen timber and stone, and returned to his stunned marine. He forced the small rifle into his hands, clasping his fingers around it as though the weapon could revive him; could resuscitate his senses.

It did. His frozen fingers clasped the dark wood of the stock as he blinked his way back into alertness. As he did, a flutter in his eyelids told Hampton that the pain had come back to him along with the memory of what had happened, of the massive devastation and unimaginable change in such a brutally short time frame. He doubled over, exposing the score mark across his right shoulder blade. Hampton fumbled at his pouches, coming out with a wound dressing which he shoved into the damaged clothing to cover as much of the injury as possible.

"We need to move, now," Hampton told him through thick lips in a voice which still didn't sound like it was his own.

"The others?" Enfield asked, barely able to keep his eyes open.

"They got away, lad. They got away."

Enfield smiled, thinking of the sweet little girl and the tough, resourceful boy.

Whatever happens to me, he thought, *at least they've got a chance.*

TWENTY

"Anything?" Johnson asked Bufford as he looked in the smashed remains of the large wing mirror.

"Nothing," he replied, "where are we going?"

"No idea," Johnson said, "just anywhere but here." Just then a loud double-thump came from the thin wall behind the cab. The others in the back wanted to stop. Johnson said nothing but drove on until he found an empty lay-by on a stretch of open road. As far as he could see, nothing could jump out on them there.

He jumped out, weapon up and ready, and rolled up the rear doors as Bufford pressed ahead to point his weapon down the road. Astrid started straight in with the questions, demanding to know where Hampton and Enfield were. Johnson just shook his head slowly, and saw her features darken and set hard.

It was her armour. She defended her soul from the devastating news by hearing it, then shutting it out of her feelings until such time that she would be able to deal with it properly. That space, that emotional void, was still occupied by the death of half her team in the cursed air insertion so long ago, and more recently when her friend Christian Berg was lost so brutally and senselessly in the helicopter crash. That space was filling with bodies fast, and she worried that it might overflow before she got the time to deal with any of it.

"Where are we going?" Kimberley asked, leaning forward to place a reassuring hand on his arm. The touch was as much to reassure her as it was him.

"I don't know," he admitted sadly, "I just don't bloody know."

———

Nevin drove in at the head of the small convoy, recovered from the ordeal of being sprayed with Michaels' brain matter and oddly pleased with himself. A sullen crowd gathered to greet their return, but the mood was less than welcoming. Two of the guards had been almost overt in their allegiance to the people there, publicly voicing their disgust at how Michaels had hunted people down like animals. The smoulder of revolt didn't take flame then, because the news of Michaels' death sent waves of shock and relief around them.

The relief was short lived, because Nevin's words made it obvious that he had chosen himself to step into the vacant shoes. He told them that they all had to move on, to carry on with their lives and ensure their survival. He reminded them that the monsters were still out there; that their safety was not guaranteed.

Then he made a mistake. He ordered for the blood and viscera to be cleaned out of the Ferret and walked away without waiting for a volunteer, just assuming that it would be done without question. He demanded fresh clothes brought to him and began stripping off as he headed inside the main building. He didn't hang around or even glance backwards to see if his instructions were being carried out, because he just assumed that he could step in where Michaels had left off.

He washed in a bowl of lukewarm water, ducking his head under and flinching as a chunk of something small and sharp jabbed painfully into his finger. He raised his head, water dripping down his eyebrows as he looked to find the source of the affliction. He picked the tiny shard of sharp bone out of his flesh, disgust and pain on his angry face despite the tiny proportions of the injury. He finished washing, looking around to see if the fresh clothes he had ordered had been delivered unobtrusively without him noticing. They hadn't, so he forced himself to put back on the boots and trousers he had worn all day. He wore the inner layers of his top half but couldn't bring himself to wear anything still matted with the partial remains of the man who had ruled the place he now saw as his own. Shivering against the cold as he wore two layers too few to stave off the low temperatures, he went back outside wearing a foul look and prepared to take his temper out on the first people he found.

He walked outside and found a gathering of people facing the entrance, milling about almost uncertainly as though they lacked the final catalyst to take action as a group. They had a clear common purpose, but the spark to ignite the flame was missing.

That spark came when a bedraggled woman gently pushed her way to the front rank and faced him down. She rubbed at her wrists where they had been tied until the revolt had forced her release. She showed no emotion when she heard the news of Michaels' death, but inside she rejoiced almost cruelly, betraying a side to her personality that she didn't know she had. She wasn't ashamed of it. Now she faced the shivering man and felt the weight of the support behind her making her more powerful than he was.

. . .

Nevin knew it in the same moment that she did, and his hand fumbled in the pocket of the trousers for the revolver. The crowd descended on him as one, pinning his arms and body with so many hands that he was utterly powerless to resist. It was the realisation that the threat of violence only held so much sway over others, and when the majority recognised their power, they were an unstoppable force. The gun was wrested from his grip and the barrel turned on him for the cold metal to grind the soft, thin layer of flesh between his eyes. He screwed his eyes shut tightly and tried to squirm away from the pressure, a keening noise escaping his mouth without permission, until a strong voice cut through the hum.

"No," she said, "not like that."

"Hang the bastard!" a woman shouted in a shrill voice made aggressive by the horrors of oppression.

"Shoot him," yelled a man, most likely unwilling or unable to do so himself, but happy to allow another to bear the burden.

"We can't let him go," another voice shouted, being met with grumbles of affirmation and support.

Pauline thought about it, thought about how best to satisfy the people who had suffered under the control and cruelty of him and people like him. The others had been given a choice; stay and become one of them or leave and consider themselves apart forever. None of them was the ringleader type, but this man, Nevin, he was toxic.

"Oh," she said nastily, letting all of the anger and frustration pour out of her after months of imprisonment, "we *can* let him go."

Nevin was frogmarched by so many pairs of hands around the building to face the sea from the high cliffs. He had begun to hope that they would banish him, would eject him from the safety of the Hilltop with only the clothes on his back. He willed them to do that, begged and pleaded in between threatening and abusing the people pinning his arms. One man pushed through to spit in his face, and looked horrified when Nevin spat back, as each man held the same contempt and hatred for the other. The man despised Nevin for what he had done to people, how he had bullied and exploited the weak. Nevin hated him because he hated everyone.

He was powerless to resist the will of the people, but babbled pleas and threats constantly in the desperate hope that something, anything he said would save his life. It didn't, and without any more words or opportunity to talk his way out of his fate, they pitched him over the side of the cliff towards the sea far below and listened as his screams faded into the sounds of the crashing waves far below.

———

Captain Palmer called a meeting. Because everyone was present, it had to be held outside in the cold in order that everyone could hear him. He told them about the safe site in Scotland, about how Britain was effectively cut off and that no help would be coming in the near future. He told them that it was their duty to get there, by any means possible, and to support the remnants of the rightful government.

"It might be *your* duty," called a voice from the crowd. Palmer could not find the face of the disembodied words, but he recognised the voice and knew it belonged to the man who had always been vocal about their plight. That vocalisation had usually been negative, and his younger brother had told him of how the man had lied about his wife being pregnant in order to try and get on board one of the rescue helicopter flights back on the island. He had struck the young officer and had looked likely to do so again until another of the civilians had intervened, but since building up the life they lived at the house, he had gathered some support among the non-military people, and even his wife had returned to his side.

"...but it's not ours," he finished amidst a chorus of agreeing murmurs.

"Very true," Palmer said, "so if anyone wishes to stay here, then we will discuss the supplies and resources to be left behind."

Bizarrely, some of the civilians untethered to the squadron by family wanted to come with them, just as the surprise of a few army families wanting to stay rocked Palmer's confidence. He saw that not as a desertion, but as a failure on his part that he did not inspire those men sufficiently to follow him. The disillusion was tempered by the reassurances of Lloyd and Downes, as well as those of his younger brother, who had become more noticeable now that the possibility of a more comfortable life peeked over the horizon. Those who wanted to stay did so out of hope that loved ones and friends had survived, and that they could be there to offer safety and assistance to those who would hopefully emerge in the spring, like daffodils.

What took two days to decide, amidst arguments and tears, was that almost fifty of them wanted to stay, wanted to take over the big house and work the farm and man the defences to keep them safe from the suspected return of the Screechers when the warm weather came back. Among those fifty were half a dozen of the squadron men, but none of the RAF crews or Royal Marines had any inclination to remain behind. The core of the squadron had remained intact, but Palmer wondered how many of those would have fallen away if they hadn't rescued their families or if those they had rescued had wanted to stay. The pull of family was a force stronger than gravity. The marines, just as the remaining helicopter crew and the SAS team, all still considered themselves deployed, more than surviving a nuclear apocalypse where the undead walked the countryside in hordes, and the only support they could count on was their own. Their units were still largely intact, and that helped maintain the cohesion between the men.

Plans were drawn up, supplies were sorted and stockpiled and the three vehicles they planned to use as their convoy were meticulously prepared and repaired by cannibalising whatever they had left. They were mindful not to leave those staying behind without the use of heavy guns, and to that end they left a handful of working squadron wagons arrayed where their guns could do the most damage to any assault by the dead or the living alike. The decision as to whom to send ahead in the helicopter, which they had checked and double checked could only manage one trip, was a difficult one.

The person they should send in charge of this detachment of the civilians should be sensible and senior enough as to have their report taken seriously but should ideally not be a man who was irreplaceable on what would very likely be an arduous and dangerous journey. Palmer had thought to send Maxwell, his interim Sergeant Major, but the man was simply too vital to the running of things to let go.

He elected eventually to send the newly-minted Sergeant Ashdown, injured horribly so long ago by the gruesome animated remains of a Royal Military Policeman, and promoted to replace Maxwell as the nominal head of Assault Troop. He travelled with his family, all of them intertwined with Maxwell's relations, and his presence satisfied Palmer that the word of the RAF crew would be supported by a sergeant. He sent three other soldiers on the helicopter, none of them carrying more than a small bag as the weight of luggage would put lives in danger in many ways, and those men were carrying some form of illness or injury that would hamper their performance on the hundreds of miles of unknown road they would likely be fighting along.

The two newest arrivals, shrouded in tragedy, had both

flatly refused to come. Both held on to the desperate belief that their loved ones were still alive, and both knew that they wouldn't find their way to the Highlands of Scotland and across a stretch of sea to find safety, so they stayed.

Arrayed the next morning before the ornate walls of the house, and seeming at odds with the building, but at home with the barbed wire and trenches, the large Bedford truck and two Fox wagons, along with the dirty Land Cruiser adopted by the SAS team, set off without fanfare or ceremony, heading north towards uncertainty. The helicopter, warmed and checked thoroughly after weeks of frozen inactivity, lifted off and thrummed sedately away into the gloomy winter sky.

Palmer, unfamiliar with the Fox but picking up the commander's seat and the controls with an ease which spoke highly of his intellect, paused before they rolled out. He looked down to the man who was staying, but who he had hoped would come. The man's loyalties ran too deep for him to abandon hope of his real boss returning.

"Corporal Daniels," Palmer said as he waved him over, "I don't suppose I can facilitate an eleventh-hour deal and convince you to join us?"

"'Fraid not, Sir," he said with a smile, "I'll stay and mind the radio. Mister Johnson will pop up again when the weather breaks, I'm sure of it."

"I pray for all our sakes, Corporal, that you are right." He leaned down, fixing the man with direct eye contact and held out a gloveless hand. Daniels climbed up on the hull of the angular wagon, removed his own woolly mitten, and took the hand in a firm grip, shaking it as the cold flesh of both men's hands warmed slightly as though the skin liked company.

"Drive safe, boss," he told him.

"You also," Palmer replied, "I'll make contact when I can, see if we can't reconnect in summer."

Daniels nodded, sure that he wouldn't see any of the men

again but feeling that he had done the right thing by staying. Someone had to keep the pilot light on for the SSM, because Daniels knew the man well enough that even if he was dead, properly dead and not one of the Screechers, then he would have spent the last moments of his life doing something worthwhile. He knew if he was still alive then he would find him, eventually, and if he was one of those things? Well if he was, then corporal Charlie Daniels would do for him personally, then follow the boys to Scotland.

On his own if he had to.

TWENTY-ONE

Nevin came to, his head unbelievably thick and groggy as he struggled to recall how he had come to be where he was. To answer that conundrum, he thought, he had to first figure out where that was in relation to where he last remembered being, and when he followed that memory-string back to the source, he recalled with horrifying clarity what had happened. They had seized him, stripped him of his gun and dragged him to the cliffs. Without mercy, much the same way that he treated people, they had thrown him off the cliff into the evening sky where he didn't so much fall as tumble, end over agonising end, until his broken body came to rest on a soft, mossy outcrop and his skull thumped hard into the natural green rug until the resistance of the rock underneath fought back and knocked him out cold.

He didn't know how long he had been unconscious, much as the way these things worked when hit very hard in the head. But his clouded mind reasoned that it hadn't grown fully dark yet, and logic dictated that given the freezing temperatures he was highly unlikely to have been unconscious all night. He reckoned he would have died of exposure if that had been the case.

As his senses slowly returned to him, he blinked his eyes to better focus on what he could see around him. A rhythmic huffing sound came from nearby, but he didn't understand what could make such a noise, and besides, the sight his eyes drank in shut off all concentration to anything else. He had lifted his head, propping himself up on one elbow to stare down the length of his body at where his legs had once been. He knew what he saw couldn't be his legs because, for one, he knew that if they were, then the sickening sight of the broken bones protruding through the pale, grey flesh and the dirty material of the trousers would prompt at least some feeling of pain. He felt nothing, and tried to move the broken leg he could see. It didn't budge, so he tried harder, grunting as he forced all of his effort into making the feet twitch, move, or do anything in response to his commands. He visually traced the feet and legs back to his own waist, patting his body as he went upwards until finally he was rewarded with the sensation of being touched at his midriff. He froze, patting downwards again and feeling nothing before moving his hands back up until he could feel his own touch. His hands moved faster, whipping up into a desperate frenzy as he sucked in a deep breath and began to scream in fear and horror and hope that the paralysis was something his brain had invented, or that he was still unconscious, but those thoughts were pushed aside as another feeling came to him.

Nails raked down his scalp from behind, making him squeal and move awkwardly as his top half dragged the numb, dead lower half with it. He turned to see, to *smell*, the rotten waste of what had once been a person wriggling towards him on the same rocky outcrop above the waves below. He shrieked, the decomposed beast shrieked back, sounding a hollow hiss in place of the characteristic scream, and the two inched closer to one another as the battered, limbless, ruined corpse shuffled inexorably closer to the paralysed man who could do nothing to defend himself but scream louder. Nevin tried to escape, tried to drag his half-useless body over the rocky green of the outcrop and drag himself clear of the rotten monstrosity that was thrashing slowly with one arm and no legs from the knees down. It must have been there for a while, because it was barely identifiable as a person other than by shape.

Nevin's numb hands slipped on the soggy, moss-covered rock, and his face hit the ground with no body strength to support him. As he hit, the cracked stumps of blackened teeth reached forwards and connected with the skin beside his right eyebrow. It clamped down, ripping and tearing as the sudden heat of his blood threatened to cook his face in contrast to the frigid air whipping around them. He howled in pain and fear as the thing craned its neck forward to chomp on his face again. He desperately tried to claw his own way to the ledge and pour himself over to dash his own body on the rocks beneath. He failed, but he did succeed in dislodging his attacker. It fell off the ledge, coming to rest only a foot below on another rock, but that distance was an insurmountable peak to the thing as it could barely locomote any more. Sudden heat, a burning intensity from within him, replaced the bracing cold he could feel. He knew the wind was still blowing hard against his exposed skin, but he no longer felt the temperature of it.

He dragged himself into a position half against the rock face, looking out over the gathering gloom and dark clouds over the English Channel. Hot blood ran down his face, and he suffered in fiery agony as the infection tore through his ruined body to finish him slowly.

As the strength fled from what was left of his body in the form of his hot blood that let off small clouds of steam as it spilled, he lapsed again into blackness as, below him, the rotten thing stopped chewing, letting the strip of flesh pulled from his face fall away, and lapsed back into its icy hibernation.

Nevin, or at least the broken thing that used to be Nevin, remained on that cliff ledge for untold months until he eventually rotted away to nothing. The last thing to die, the infected core of his brainstem, lay dormant as the body that carried it was useless. Nevin never took another life, never had the chance to spread fear and infection as he had when he was counted among the living, and he was forced to watch the coming and going of the tide on an island he no longer had the capacity to understand.

———

Above him, on the day after he had been rejected from the human race for non-compliance, a pair of eyes looked down on his immobile body from a deeply lined face. The face was lined with age, but mostly with worry and stress after a lifetime spent organising the activities of others. Those eyes had driven through appalling weather conditions, nursing the ungainly box truck at often very low speeds until they had seen the tell-tale column of smoke coming from a building high on a hill-top. They had reached it eventually, spending three long hours watching it for signs of hostility before driving up the steep approach road. When the occupants of that hilltop bastion took in their weapons and remains of uniform, they had pointed their shotguns and rifles at them.

Johnson and Bufford, the only ones visible as the others were in the breezy back of the truck, did little to assuage their fears that they weren't hostile, but when the two women and the two children climbed down from the back, suddenly the atmosphere changed for the better. The woman who seemed to be in charge of them bustled to the front and brought them inside to feed them, providing hot drinks almost constantly and marvelling at the bearded man's capacity to guzzle down coffee, and she spoke to them about what had happened to bring their two groups together. It soon became clear that people from this camp had attacked them, but as three of the exhausted newcomers snatched up their weapons, seemingly expecting to fight again, she had assured them that the time of their existence when they hurt other people was well and truly over.

"Those men are gone now," she assured them, "one never came back and the other we dealt with ourselves."

That was when they had been shown the carnage of blood and gore inside the Ferret. That was when Johnson had been shown the place where the man called Nevin had been tossed off the cliff as a definitive sign that he was unwelcome.

The woman, Pauline, was wary of scaring the two children but was very attentive to them and their needs. She asked them their names, and the young boy answered for them.

"She doesn't talk much," he explained with a sad, depreciating smile, "not since her mum got taken away by bad men."

Something about what he said struck a chord cold in Pauline's heart, and her gasp as her hand fluttered at her mouth made everyone sit up and take notice.

"What is your mummy's name?" she said in a voice affected solely for addressing a frightened young girl.

Amber looked at her, then at Peter, then back the woman who asked the obviously silly question. She leaned in and whispered to Peter, the only way she would still communicate with anyone other than him, by using the older boy as a medium. He smiled, looked back at Pauline and answered for Amber.

"She said she's called 'Mummy'…"

Pauline smiled despite her frustration and tried another way.

"Do people call her Ellie?"

The mention of the name flashed across Amber's eyes like electricity, and she began to look around as her young brain associated knowledge of her mother to the possibility of her being there. She didn't see her, obviously, but her wide eyes turned back to Pauline and pleaded for her to tell her where her mother was. The older woman's eyes fell, crushing her with the knowledge that she would have to be the bearer of bad news and break the girl's heart all over again.

"I'm really sorry... *Amber*," she said warily, reaching out for the girl's hand and trying not to take offense when she snatched it away. "She was here until two days ago, but we tried to run away from the bad people who were here before. They caught me and brought me back, but Ellie... but your mum she..." Pauline cuffed away the tears rolling down her cheeks as she looked into the bright, wide eyes of the little girl who mirrored her tears in utter silence.

"Your mum wasn't caught, so she must have got away with another little girl called Jessica."

At the mention of the other name, the little boy started. His gasp was exaggerated and drawn out, becoming a whining noise which morphed into words seamlessly as he spoke in rapid excitement.

"Jessica? How old is she? What did she look like?"

Pauline held up both hands to calm the innocent onslaught of his questions before she answered.

"She's a teenager," she told him, "slim and quiet with long, brown hair."

"Has she got..." Peter hesitated, embarrassed of the facts behind what he was admitting but knowing that it would solve the confusion unquestioningly, "has she got scars on her..." his voice trailed away again but his fingers mimed slices across his wrist. Pauline's mouth dropped open, as though the chances of finding one of the missing children she knew about was huge, but both was unbelievable. Her reaction gave flame to the kindling of Peter's stress and fear and hope and he burst out in tears, falling down to the ground and sobbing as Amber, silent tears still streaming down her cheeks, dropped down behind him to wrap him in a hug that melted the hearts of even the toughest human beings to witness it.

Johnson coughed, clearing his throat and turning away from the scene as Kimberley met his eyes. She cried, emotions of the past months boiling out of her at the display of innocence and humanity, and she wrapped her arms around his neck where the relief and sadness just flowed. Beside them Astrid wiped her eyes clear of tears as her own, but Bufford remained staunch and silent.

"I've got to find her," Peter cried, his own upset making Amber cry louder and harder with him. People crowded the children, eager to comfort them and mistaking them for helpless dependants instead of the tough, resourceful survivors they were.

"We will, Peter," Johnson told him from behind Kimberley's embrace, "I promise we will." He meant it and eyed the half-covered hull of the Warrior fighting vehicle Michaels had emplaced and knew just how useful the new technology would be to enable him to make that promise become a reality.

TWENTY-TWO

Mike Xavier took over on watch, adjusting the grip on his fire axe as he switched his head from right to left. He could hear his heart beat in his ears, and each breath made him worry that the sound of his rising panic would bring down an unstoppable horde of undead to tear them apart.

He was a calm leader. He had faced off with corrupt officials in foreign countries, had braved countless weather fronts capable of killing him and his crew, had worked in conditions so treacherous in his rise to captaincy that he would have thought himself better equipped than he was to deal with this unexpected hell. He was learning more about himself, and what he was learning wasn't filling him with confidence about his abilities.

He had taken over from the diminutive Canadian woman, Philippa, on guard duty as they ran short shuttle runs to bring back the stocks of food they had found a dozen miles down the river. The thickly populated areas showed few or no lights, but Xavier's upbringing on the banks of the Mersey had left him with an almost telepathic intuition about the area. He had directed them to hit the shoreline near to a golf course on the opposite bank and there they had pillaged the store room of an abandoned club house before loading as many crates as they could of food and bottles of drink on board the four electric golf buggies they had borrowed for the task. They drove their supplies down to the river and loaded them on board the small fishing craft before returning twice to take more. It was on that third return trip when they had just got back to the boat and he had taken over sentry duty as two others had done before him, when they came at them from the darkness.

Emerging in a ghostly formation from the inky black beyond the reach of the weak light still glowing on the jetty they occupied, a dozen undead shuffled on damaged bodies and chilled feet towards them uncertainly. He didn't know what it was that had attracted them.

The smell of us? Or have we made more noise than we think we have? Christ, it's like they have a sixth bloody sense of where we are...

"Get back on the boat," he hissed.

"Two, maybe three more trips," Jean-Pierre told him in a voice that was a force of magnitude too loud for Xavier's comfort. The sweat on his palms doubled before he could answer.

"Sshhh! For fuck's sake! Get back here."

The desperation in his tone cut through to Jean-Pierre like a blade. He froze, having the good sense not to drop his burden, but gently bend his legs and sink down to rest it on the ground silently. He paced fast to his right, taking three quiet strides until he blocked the path of their stocky mechanic and whispered in his ear. Jase dropped his burden, less quietly, and fast walked towards the boat as though not looking around would render him invisible to the things that hunted them.

"What the hell?" came a loud and annoyed Canadian voice from the darkness, "Who the heck is leaving their stuff in the dark? I could'a fallen over that, you know? Could'a hurt myself real bad."

Three desperate voices shushed her in response. Philippa froze, hearing a guttural shriek pierce the air in the near pitch black. Other shrieks joined in, firing off in yelping barks like urban foxes heard in the dead of night, only they all knew there were no foxes there making that noise. The three of them still a way from the short jetty froze, huddling together in fear. From his position higher up, and having been in the darkness longer than the others and still in possession of his full night vision abilities, Mike Xavier watched as the loose line of zombies stopped. The one at the centre of the line, the one he thought looked like a leader as it was the first to move before the others fell in with it, barked another long shriek again and slowly turned its head in a very specific direction.

Directly towards Jason, Jean-Pierre, and Philippa McAndrew.

"Ruuuun," he bawled, dropping down heavily onto the surface of the wooden platform before he chopped down with the blade of his axe on the mooring line to sever it instantly.

He heard the thudding of feet in the cold, still air, but what separated his own people from the undead was that one set of thumping footfalls came with the rasping of desperate and terrified breathing, whereas the other did not. The living ran towards him just as fast as the dead did, and it was a straight race as to who would arrive first.

He fired up the engine, revving it into life and not caring who or what heard any more because they'd already been discovered, and were already being hunted by a pack of them.

Two thuds sounded impossibly loud on their ungainly and borderline overloaded boat, followed by a third who shouted, "Go, go!" as he sailed through the air to almost collide with Xavier at the controls.

They pushed off, accelerating to loop out away from the muddy shoreline and into the deeper water of the channel. As he pulled away, Xavier dared risk a look back as splash after

splash sounded over the roar of the tiny engine and he looked
to see the vague hints of human shapes dropping off the jetty
towards them. The animated dead bodies sank, lacking the
buoyancy and speed of movement to swim, but one remained
standing resolute on the jetty. It was so calm, its gaze so intent
and almost *knowing*, that Mike throttled back to look at it.

He knew from seeing their eyes up close that there was no
way it could see him, no way those milky eyes could focus at
distance in the dark and find him, yet the thing seemed to be
staring directly through his soul. With a long, hissing shriek it
turned away, and all of the others who hadn't fallen into the
freezing water turned to follow him a second later.

Silence hung on their small, stolen boat as none of them
wanted to be the first to speak. None of them wanted to ask
how the shuffling blind things had found them, how they had
screamed into the air and somehow known precisely where
they were. None of them wanted to ask why they had seemed
to be following the orders of one of them, for fear of sounding
insane, but all of them were thinking it.

On the plus side, they had recovered more food in the few
hours they had been away than the entire failed foray into the
city had yielded in its entirety. Mike was happy with that, as
food was the great leveller when it came to dealing with
hungry, scared people. So, as they settled in for their slow
return journey north towards the mouth of the estuary by the
docks housing their beloved *Maggie,* he concentrated on the
rolling blackness of the water and tried to block out the
thoughts that threatened to overcome him with dread and
desperation.

The sun was beginning to rise as they returned, casting a
ghostly ethereal glow on the far side of his ship's huge profile.
The mist hung in great swirls, occasionally obscuring the
skyline of the city behind the docks. One swirl of chilly white
cloud parted ahead of them, and a gasp from the bow of their

small craft made Xavier throttle back to nothing to investigate. He dashed forwards to see Philippa, one hand clasped to her mouth, pointing to the water ahead.

A body, face down in the classic dead man's float, bobbed in the swell ahead. The jacket it wore was bloated with trapped air, but the immobility and the deathly stillness of the body made it clear that it had been in the cold water for too long to waste their efforts by getting whoever it was out. They exchanged looks in the gloom of the pre-dawn, eyes like white beacons in their cold faces, and heads were shaking to indicate the sentiment of being unable to save them.

As the mist swirled and cleared on the approach to the huge vertical wall that was their floating fortress, a shriek erupted from high above them. They all froze, knowing that sound and hearing it on an almost cellular level as every inch of their bodies reacted instinctively in fear. As the adrenaline coursed through them, the sound reverberated around the abandoned docks and gave a chilling doppler effect as the person issuing the shriek plummeted overboard to fly like a house brick straight down.

The noise of the body hitting the water was like an explosion, and the icy water splashing over them took away the breath of the two who were unaccustomed to being assaulted by the cold of the sea. All around them other shrieks pierced the air, and further ahead, more splashes sounded as fountains of white water burst upwards. From those impacts in the water, nothing surfaced. No bodies broke the surface to gasp in huge lungfuls of precious, life-giving air.

Without warning or explanation Xavier gunned the engine of their small, overloaded craft and took them out to the deeper water where he turned the boat in a wide U shape. He killed the revs again, all four of them standing and holding on to look back at the docks as the sun broke rank to peer over the top of the ship.

All of them were there. Even from the distance they were at, Mike and Jean-Pierre could recognise some of their crew, their friends, from the shapes of their bodies. But not from how they moved, because their movements were jerky and spasmodic as though they were being propelled by electrical impulses controlled by unpractised hands.

"They aren't like the ones in the city," Jean-Pierre said slowly.

"No," Philippa answered, surprising Xavier who hadn't even known she had gone on the failed expedition, "these are... *newer* somehow."

"They're not frozen up yet," Mike answered without emotion, "not like the older ones. I bet they're still warm."

His revelation quieted them all down to watch in near stunned silence as the people they had shared their space with for months, the people they had spoken to that same day, were gone. They weren't themselves any more. They were dead, but still there. Present but vacant. Moving but no longer alive. They stared for a long time, even past the time when some of their deathly pale former friends had stopped making the hideous screaming noise and scanning around for them. Long past when they had not thrown themselves overboard but simply walked off the edge of the tall deck to try and get to them. They drifted away, all but two who stared directly at them with their heads cocked slightly to one side as a dog would when waiting for a tasty morsel.

"We need to go," Philippa said, snapping them all out of their stunned reverie, "we need to find somewhere to hold up."

"What about *The Maggie*?" Jean-Pierre asked Xavier, turning to speak to him alone as he stared hard into the eyes of his captain.

"She's lost, JP," he said flatly, "and we can't keep her afloat with just the four of us anyways."

Jean-Pierre accepted the sad fate and loss of his home in

silence. Xavier said nothing, simply turned their nose around to face back down the river and opened the throttle enough to get them moving gently and not generate a loud noise for the dead to follow.

They headed inland, away from the dangers of the sea and the warships that lurked off shore. Away from the big container ship and everything they owned. Away towards uncertainty. Away towards risk and adversity, with only the food they had found, the clothes on their backs and the makeshift weapons they clutched in cold, tired hands.

TWENTY-THREE

Charlie Daniels had half a dozen soldiers left with him, and although only a corporal he was the ranking man remaining at the big house. He did what he could, setting out his stall to the thirty people left there and asking them all to do their part to make it work. Large parts of the house were shut off, it being pointless to keep them open just to allow the draught to permeate the rest of the house. They contracted to the rooms nearest the kitchen, not even bothering with the second floor of the house any longer. The small amount of livestock they had left was housed in the wide inner courtyard which was destined to become a vegetable garden as soon as the weather thawed. The nearby farm still had to be visited when the fresh vegetables were needed, but essentially with fewer than a third of their number remaining, life was significantly easier, especially as their stores would stretch to fulfill their requirements for winter, and then some.

The place had taken on an almost eerie feel, like a ghost ship or a deserted town, and no sooner had the helicopter taken off in a swirling maelstrom of whipped-up snow and the others left by vehicle, than the power struggle began.

"We need one person on watch each night," he said, "but everyone else needs to know what to do if the alarm is raised. In the daytimes we need to keep on top of the food and the firewood, but also we need to keep going out to look for other people who might have survived the wint…"

"Who died and left you in charge?" asked a whining yet deep voice. With such a small group remaining, the speaker couldn't hide, but it was the same vocal man who had tried and failed to upstage the captain when he spoke to them. It was the same man who seemed to be at the heart of every shred of disharmony, every hint of discord, and Daniels knew that he had to be dealt with before he made a play for control that he likely couldn't handle. He had to nip this in the bud, but without using force. He had to show that he was a better candidate for leadership than the budding communist in their midst.

"Nobody died," Daniels answered as though the question was a genuine one, "not recently, at least. What would *you* suggest we do?"

All eyes turned to the man, Gordon, who for a man who liked to use his above average height to intimidate people, seemed to visibly shrink a couple of sizes. Daniels executed it perfectly, as the onus was on the man for solutions instead of problems.

He had clearly stepped outside of his comfort zone. The silence was deafening, and it seemed to oppress him as though an entire football stadium had suddenly shut up just to hear the empty words he yelled at the players.

"Well, I…" Gordon said, realising that his only skill for public oration was to point out the flaws in other people's plans and not come up with any of his own, "I think we should… well, we should…"

"Exactly," Daniels said cutting him off, "that's a great idea. So," he said addressing them all again, "as my pal here has pointed out, we need to stay warm, stay fed and stay ready to defend ourselves. Everyone okay with that?"

They were. One of the civilians who stayed behind, unsurprisingly a farmer as they existed in a huge swathe of rich farmland, had offered to take the lead with the horticultural matters. Another had offered the services of him and his wife to look after the small amount of livestock they had, and both of these offers were well received. The wives, falling into the status quo of gender stereotypes, took up residence in the kitchen where the warm hearth tended by Denise Maxwell and her followers was kept alive.

Daniels wished he had managed to keep her, along with her husband of course, but he knew that his choice to stay behind in the hope that the Squadron Sergeant Major was still out there somewhere would be a lonely one.

It really was easier with fewer people there, and if anything, the house was too big for their needs. Thoughts of moving elsewhere were abandoned as pointless, and there were so many plans to make and consider that his head was spinning. He set the guard for the night, having walked the defences out in front of the house for nothing much more than something to do, and he went to spend his evening sitting in the only environment he really felt comfortable in.

He climbed inside the Sultan, left parked in the expanse of the inner courtyard half transformed into their vegetable garden, settled into the uncomfortable canvas seat, careful not to spill the cocoa in his tin mug, and twiddled with the dials to listen in on different channels as though the repetition of old habits could bring him comfort.

———

"Charlie?" a voice shouted, startling him awake inside the chilly metal coffin. He had fallen asleep in there, kept warm by the auxiliary heater despite the uncomfortable seat, which spoke of how exhausted both physically and emotionally he was.

"In here," he yelled, looking up at the closed hatch and mentally tutting at himself that the sound wouldn't carry well. He stood and opened it, popping his head out and repeating his words. The chill morning air hit him hard after a night spent slightly warmer than was comfortable.

"Incoming," the excited young trooper shouted, turning and running for the house as soon as he had passed his message. Daniels flew from the hatch of the Sultan like a grenade had just been dropped inside. So many thoughts and questions came to him – how many, what direction, how far away – but with nobody there to ask he just gripped his Sterling submachine gun and sprinted on stiff legs for the door. He burst through the house, other men throwing on heavy coats and smocks with weapons in hand ranging from their own automatic guns to shotguns used for hunting, and they jostled for position to get outside.

"Contact ahead," shouted a trooper looking through binoculars, "on the road."

"How many?" Daniels asked, the first question firing off from a list that had grown since he first heard the news.

"One," came the reply, "looks like… like a bloody *Montego!*"

"A what?" Daniels asked, his slightly muddled brain trying to figure out how the Screechers had got their hands on the off-beige car he could now see approaching them.

"It's weaving a bit," the report carried on, "two inside from what I can see…"

"Stand to, stand to!" Daniels yelled, scattering the few trained men he had into defensive positions and confusing the civilians holding their shotguns until they hesitantly followed the soldiers and took up defensive positions. They waited, peering over the sights of their weapons at the car meandering its way towards them. It came on slowly, uncertainly and with a high-pitched sound of a revving engine in need of a higher gear. Daniels, amateur mechanic as everyone in the squadron had to be, guessed that it was probably a clutch synchromesh issue, and the driver had managed to get the car moving in gear and didn't want to jeopardise their forward momentum by trying to be clever and selecting third when second kept them moving.

The car came to an abrupt stop, bumping nose first into a fence post and knocking it down before the driver overcorrected with an exaggerated snatch at the wheel to pitch them off the road into the shallower part of a ditch. Daniels stood, already running to them to offer help, as he shouted a warning to the others to keep their eyes open for bites.

When he yanked open the rear door behind the passenger, he froze. Slumped forwards, a mess of filthy camouflage uniform and assorted weapons, were two marines bleeding from half a dozen injuries.

"Sar'nt Hampton?" Daniels asked with disbelief, "what the bloody hell have you been up to?"

"Get him out," Bill Hampton said as he fluttered a weak hand at the unconscious passenger. His eyes were rolling back in his head, a mixture of concussion and exhaustion combining to rob him of his consciousness. Daniels went to the far side of the vehicle and pulled open the dented door to reach in and retrieve the marine sniper they had thought lost to them, along with others. As he reached in, a bolt of fur shot past so quickly that he couldn't tell if it was brown or black or grey. Dismissing their third feline passenger for the time being and knowing that it would gnaw at him later, he dragged the bleeding Royal Marine out and yelled for others to help him. They were both carried, hands under armpits and gloves gripping trouser legs above their boots, into the house ahead of

Daniels, who was left to retrieve the weapons from the car. A curious noise and a sensation not felt for many months nagged at his ankles and looking down, he saw the exposed back end of a cat that had its tail held high like a vehicle antenna. It snaked between his legs, coursing between them in an endless figure of eight like the symbol for infinity, and the rattling purr drifted up to him.

"Alright," he told it, "there's food inside."

As though understanding him, or at least acknowledging that he had noticed it, the cat abandoned its racetrack around the man's ankles and trotted away after the two men being hoisted up and carried.

————

The men were uninfected, which had been the primary concern especially for the seemingly negative contingent of the civilian population, and their injuries had been treated as well as they could manage. Mostly they were suffering from exhaustion and exposure, so getting them clean and warm was the best way to deal with them. Both men slept on mattresses dragged in front of a fire kept well stocked with the split logs of the ash tree in what had been the captain's office. They slept through the following day until Hampton woke first and sat up groggily to try and clear his head. A large, grazed lump was raised up on the back of his skull and had clearly affected his ability to balance.

"You should rest, Sarge," Daniels told him.

"No," Hampton answered as he checked over the sleeping marine beside him, "I need a bloody drink." Daniels didn't think that was a very good idea, but then again neither was disagreeing with the man.

"No," he insisted, "you need rest."

"See these, lad?" Hampton asked, pointing two fingers on

his left hand to his right sleeve, "these mean I tell you what to do, and you do it." His eyes looked down to where his fingers rested, and instead of seeing the chevrons of his rank displayed he saw only the cold, bruised flesh of his upper arm.

"Ah, bollocks," he said, dropping back down to the bed.

One of the women brought out a bottle from somewhere and used the tail of her apron to wipe clean a cup before pouring a decent glug and handing it to him. He took a sip, making an appreciative sounding grunt as he rolled it around his mouth and swallowed it. He looked up at Daniels, evidently assessing the man and showing neither disapproval or any sign of being impressed.

"You in charge then?"

"I suppose I am," Daniels said.

"And the others? My Lieutenant?"

Daniels told him everything. About the helicopter evacuations, the failed resupply mission at the base, the winter and the shortage of food, then the announcement of the others up in Scotland. Hampton stopped him there, firing off a few questions about specifics; location, numbers, defences, before letting him resume. That led up to their arrival and Hampton was invited to reciprocate with their own story.

It was his turn to tell them everything. He recounted the helicopter crash, where so many brave men had fought through hell only to lose their lives in a bloody accident. The unfairness of it still stung him, and he shot a cautious glance at Enfield who still slept on his side with the puckered skin of the bullet score mark exposed on his right shoulder. He told Daniels about how the other half that particular equation had been lost; how he had found marine Leigh concertinaed with a crushed spine in the wreckage of the twisted airframe. He told them of the survivors, having to raise his voice to tell the excited corporal to wait after he had erupted on hearing Johnson's name. He had to explain who Astrid Larsen was, as much as he knew anyway, and filled them in on the kids they had found living alone in all of the shit they had been wading through for months.

"Kids," he told them, "little kids all on their own and doing just fine before we turned up."

Then he crushed the re-inflated hopes of the army corporal and told them about the attack on their village. He told them about the savagery of the armoured gun rolling through their little hiding place and tearing down buildings with automatic fire. He said how he and Enfield had stayed and fired on the attackers to distract them long enough for Johnson and the others to get away. How they had come to after both thinking they would be paying the ultimate price only to find themselves banged up and all alone.

Going from elated to crushed once more, Daniels left them alone to eat and recover.

He busied himself for the rest of the day, trying to avoid too many questions so as not to have to give answers which depressed him, and when darkness threatened, he retreated to his place of comfort once more. His turning of dials was less enthusiastic than it had been the previous evening as the man he had hoped to make contact with was missing, with God knew what chasing him. The location Hampton had given them was half a day away in the snow at least, and from there he was so far behind their scent that attempting to track them down was less than pointless. He lapsed into a catatonic state of immobility, numb to everything including the cold coming in through the open hatch with a view to preventing him from falling asleep there again. A crackle of static came from one of the battered radio headphones left resting on the hook where they hung. Daniels looked at it, willing it to speak to him again and not believing that he hadn't imagined it. He glanced away, convincing himself that the sound was in his head. It crackled again, too low to hear but rolling in a pattern that made him think of familiar words. He snatched them up, leaning forwards to grab them and force them over his head.

The sounds of the outside world went quiet, blocked out and replaced only with the rapid sounds of his breathing. Nothing happened, and his finger hovered of the transmit button before he took it away and reached up to pull off the headphones, annoyed with himself for allowing his imagination to interrupt normal programming. Just as he went to sack the activity as pointless, the noise came back to him loud and clear.

"Hello, any station, this is Foxtrot-three-three-alpha…" came a slow, almost bored sounding voice, as though the message had been repeated ad infinitum and no longer held any passion.

Daniels was certain that he had imagined it. There was no way that could be genuine.

"Hello, any station, any station, this is Foxtrot-three-three-alpha…"

Daniels stabbed his finger onto the transmit button and croaked out a response without allowing his voice to settle to its normal radio tone.

"Foxtrot-three-three-alpha, this is zero-bravo," he said, snatching at the vehicle callsign from a lifetime ago, "is it really you?"

A pause on the other end made him doubt that he had heard it at all, that he was asleep and dreaming it.

———

"It's really me," Johnson said from fifty miles away sat in the slightly roomier and far more modern interior of the Warrior sat on the hilltop over the cliffs by the English Channel, "and, my God, it's good to hear your voice."

TWENTY-FOUR

The first day's progress was pretty poor, Palmer had to admit. They had encountered too many obstacles and turned around too many times to make any distance, and their path north on the wider roads was blocked by a frozen shattered barricade of ruined bodies stretching out as far as they could see. The carnage was horrendous, but at least they were spared the stench that would probably be detectable from space when the weather warmed up again. There was no way through, and by nightfall on their first day they had barely made two hundred miles after having to backtrack and avoid the obstacle of dead.

They circled their wagons as such, occupying an empty building for a restless and uncomfortable night.

The following morning they were forced to keep to the smaller roads, which halved their average speed. The following day went better than the first, with Sergeant Strauss ranging ahead to scout the best path before the heavy truck followed under escort of the other Fox and the battered-looking Land Cruiser adopted by the SAS men. Fuel was found when they ran dry, but they had brought enough food carried by them individually that they weren't forced to scavenge. Everywhere there was evidence of hordes having passed through, where entire wide swathes of landscape still showed signs of having been trampled flat by thousands of pairs of undead feet.

"Choke point ahead," Strauss reported via radio, "too narrow for the Bedford."

"Can you force it?" Palmer asked, feeling the pregnancy of the pause as the question was considered.

"Roger," the response came.

Ahead, peering out of the limited viewing slit of the Fox, Strauss instructed his driver to slowly force the truck blocking their path out of the way. Being unable to get through the village would mean a long detour and another hour turning around to backtrack and locate an alternative route.

"Easy," Strauss cautioned, "don't damage us…"

As soon as he had issued the warning, the truck blocking the way shunted forward with a metallic crack followed by a creaking noise as the snapped handbrake cable could no longer arrest the momentum of the heavy vehicle. It rolled, gathering speed on the very shallow slope, and crashed into the glass front of a building.

It was a cinema, only a small one but one which had been occupied when an infected person staggered inside to flee the horrors on the street. Everyone inside had been turned, and as none of them retained enough fine motor control to operate the fiddly door locks, that was where they remained until the sound of shattering glass woke them from the state of inactivity they had all fallen into. As though heat radiated through them and melted their coma-like states, the noise woke them in waves and sparked their animation until they all funnelled out of the building and turned their ashen faces and clouded eyes towards the main attraction: the sound of an engine and a moving vehicle.

"Fall back," Strauss yelled, startled by the sudden appear-ance of so many undead heading directly for them from close range. His driver threw the wagon into reverse and propelled them backwards as Strauss shouted the warning over the radio.

Hearing the news of a mass of dead directly ahead, the first they had encountered other than one or two half-frozen Screechers posing little or no threat, Palmer roared for the rest of his convoy to stand-to. The radio sparked into life again, this time Strauss giving them the bad news that in their haste to withdraw backwards, his driver had beached them on the wrecked remains of a car.

"Get clear, leave us," Strauss instructed. Palmer had no intention of abandoning any of his men, regardless of how long for, and he ordered everyone out to form line.

Like some echo of infantry from hundreds of years prior, Palmer lined the men up shoulder to shoulder to face the onslaught and slug it out toe-to-toe.

"Make ready," he ordered loudly as he pushed himself into the very centre of their line and extend the stock of his Sterling, "aim…"

As one, all of the assorted weaponry of his men drew up level to aim at the oncoming undead who advanced with their mouths open to emit the hideous shriek that had earned them their nickname. Their musty stench ranged ahead of them like a picquet, turning the noses of the armed men and threatening to double them over in repulsion ahead of the main wave of attack.

Palmer filled his lungs, intending to call the order to fire loudly and whip his men into action. Before he could give the order, a great bark of diesel engine filled the air as a main battle tank, huge and loud in the confines of the town's streets, revved and rolled towards them on squeaking tracks. Stunned, the dismounted men held their fire and stared in confused awe at the arrival of such a heavy hitter, then watched as it spun on its tracks to turn up the road and rolled forward again, straight into the advancing enemy to crush them down under its sixty-tonne weight. It went ahead, stopping when the tidal wave of undead ran dry, cracked off two short bursts from the mounted MG3 similar to their own GPMGs. The clattering gun went silent as quickly as it had started, and the tank clunked into reverse to go back over the crushed wave of stinking corpses.

"Give them room," Palmer instructed, dispersing his men so that they didn't become living victims of the unfamiliar heavy killer. The tank stopped, nudging its bulk to the side to shunt the stranded Fox off the wrecked vehicle carcass it had bellied out on, like a larger tortoise stopping to nudge a smaller one free of a troublesome rock, then it continued backwards to stop near the rest of the convoy. The hatch opened, and up popped a crisply overalled man with a moustache and a black beret adorned with a silver badge of the tank he commanded.

He climbed down, stamping to attention as the heels of his boots clacked together.

"Good afternoon," he announced in accented English, "Hauptmann Hans Wolff."

Palmer took a stunned step forwards, lowering his weapon and raising his hand to return the salute that the man was offering.

"Captain Julian Simpkins-Palmer," he answered, unsure what was happening, "how did you… where did…"

Wolff smiled, disarming his English counterpart.

"Captain," he said, "we hear you would be heading this way and we have been intending to do the same."

"From who?"

Wolff held up a hand to calm the questioning.

"I apologise, Captain, perhaps I should be starting in the beginning?"

———

Barrett's tired Sea King flared in to land on the flat surface directly outside the small control tower of Broadford airfield. Designed for small, light aircraft only, the navy pilot was shocked to see the dull green fuselage of heavier military transport planes, and could only imagine the high-stakes pressure of that landing, which would only be described as 'tactical' as the pilot pretty much slammed the plane on the deck and hauled on full reverse to save over running the small stretch of tarmac. On their swoop in he saw what looked like ground works going on to extend the runway, and that kind of investment made him feel happier that this place was designed to stay infection free.

They were met at gunpoint. Nothing overly hostile, but the intention to use the arrayed weapons was clear.

"Nothing to be alarmed about," called a gruff but cultured male voice via a loudspeaker horn, "we need to observe quarantine rules first."

Men in biohazard suits came forward, ushering the helicopter passengers away one by one as they were led inside to be stripped, checked, given a fresh jumpsuit and left behind clear plastic curtains where large metal urns bubbled ready for their hot drinks.

Barrett, Sergeant Ashdown and the rest of his crew in tow, called out for the officer in charge.

"That would be me," said the man with the speaker, "Colonel Kelly, British Army." He wore a sandy brown beret with the famous winged dagger badge visible as it reflected the weak sunlight. Barrett replied with his own rank, introducing the others with him.

"We'll catch up when you've been processed, Barrett," Kelly said, turning away.

They waited their turn, going into another plastic curtained room to strip off and leave their clothing to be burned. The civilians had no issue with this, but the men of Her Majesty's forces were a little more precious over giving up their uniform. They were assured that they would get replacements, but their reluctance was made worse when they went through to the larger waiting area and found themselves wearing the same plain coveralls as the civilians. Their bearing marked them out as military, and Colonel Kelly approached them on the other side of the thick, clear plastic.

"Gentlemen," he greeted them before he was interrupted by a loud voice.

"Now look here, man," crowed the voice of their own Colonel, the half-insensible man from a Scottish regiment, who probably hadn't seen any real soldiering since the Korean War, "tell your man to give me back my father's claymore!"

Kelly looked at him, glancing back to Barrett and receiving an apologetic shrug by way of explanation, before ignoring the man as an insignificance.

"Major Downes didn't come with you?" he asked the pilot.

"Not enough room on board and not enough fuel for two trips, Sir," he answered. Kelly nodded.

"So, they're travelling by road then?" Barrett nodded through the plastic curtain in response.

"The Wolfpack?" a junior officer asked Kelly.

"Wolfsrudel," he responded, correcting him with a smirk, "but yes, please do put them on alert." He turned back to the quarantined men and added, "one hour in here, then you'll come with me to our HQ to be debriefed." He announced it as though it was already fact, as though it was written in stone because he had decided it. He gave off an air of arrogance, but one matched with a brutal competence and confidence in his abilities and the abilities of his men that such arrogance was almost instantly forgiven.

"But I warn you, gentlemen," he said ominously, "the situation may not be as rosy as you were hoping for."

EPILOGUE

"Doc, are you certain that you can create more of the virus from the research material the Brits recovered from your lab?" drawled the man in the grey suit with an accent that could only be narrowed down to somewhere on the lower east coast.

Professor Sunil Grewal bit back the correction that he hadn't been a mere doctor for over ten years. Something told him that the man in the very plain suit with the very plain face wouldn't have cared anyway. The men and women of the CIA all had one thing in common when it came to him; none of them seemed to give much of a damn about what he said or thought, only what he could do.

"I am certain that I can," he said, "but the question remains of why you would want me to."

The suit didn't answer his question, but simply turned away and gestured at the doorway where another suit was bringing in a bespectacled man in a lab coat, clutching a leather satchel to his chest. Everything about him said that he wasn't there by choice.

"Doc Grewal, Doc Chambers," the suit said, introducing them. Grewal knew of Professor Richard Chambers by reputation. He was an immunologist who had spent most of his life working on vaccines. Scientifically speaking, the two men were opposite sides of a coin; Chambers had devoted his life to stopping nature's destructive will, whereas Grewal had enhanced and weaponised it. The two professors nodded a wary greeting at one another, as though they were both waiting for the punchline, when the suits began to file out of the lab.

"Make more of it, then figure out how to kill it. The president needs a vaccine in a month to start rolling out production. Make no mistake, gentlemen, it's not a case of *if* this virus reaches the United States but *when*. I suggest you use your time wisely."

With that, he left and shut the door. Through the glass section Grewal could see the uniformed guard standing mutely in place. He turned to Professor Dick Chambers, holding out a hand to be shook and opened his mouth to speak.

Chambers hit him in the face with a nervous and tentative right-handed jab, shocking them both. He hit him again, harder this time as his confidence grew, and rocked the man back on his feet. He hit him a third time, dropping his satchel and putting his body weight into the blow to knock the other scientist off his feet to land hard on his backside.

Grewal dabbed a hand to his face, feeling lips already swelling and taking his fingertips away from his nose covered in a film of oily blood.

"Are you finished?" he asked as he looked up at the tearful, red face of his attacker.

"Yes," Chambers said, "now show me what ungodly mutation you've cooked up, and I can see if I can undo your goddamned Frankenstein's mess."

ALSO IN THE SERIES

.

FROM THE PUBLISHER

Thank you for reading *Adversity,* the fourth of six books in Toy Soldiers.

We hope you enjoyed it as much as we enjoyed bringing it to you. We just wanted to take a moment to encourage you to review the book on Amazon and Goodreads. Every review helps further the author's reach and, ultimately, helps them continue writing fantastic books for us all to enjoy.

If you liked this book, check out the rest of our catalogue at www.aethonbooks.com. To sign up to receive a FREE collection from some of our best authors as well as updates regarding all new releases, visit www.aethonbooks.com/sign-up.

SPECIAL THANKS TO:

ADAWIA E. ASAD	EDDIE HALLAHAN	KYLE OATHOUT
JENNY AVERY	JOSH HAYES	LILY OMIDI
BARDE PRESS	PAT HAYES	TROY OSGOOD
CALUM BEAULIEU	BILL HENDERSON	GEOFF PARKER
BEN	JEFF HOFFMAN	NICHOLAS (BUZ) PENNEY
BECKY BEWERSDORF	GODFREY HUEN	JASON PENNOCK
BHAM	JOAN QUERALTÓ IBÁÑEZ	THOMAS PETSCHAUER
TANNER BLOTTER	JONATHAN JOHNSON	JENNIFER PRIESTER
ALFRED JOSEPH BOHNE IV	MARCEL DE JONG	RHEL
CHAD BOWDEN	KABRINA	JODY ROBERTS
ERREL BRAUDE	PETRI KANERVA	JOHN BEAR ROSS
DAMIEN BROUSSARD	ROBERT KARALASH	DONNA SANDERS
CATHERINE BULLINER	VIKTOR KASPERSSON	FABIAN SARAVIA
JUSTIN BURGESS	TESLAN KIERINHAWK	TERRY SCHOTT
MATT BURNS	ALEXANDER KIMBALL	SCOTT
BERNIE CINKOSKE	JIM KOSMICKI	ALLEN SIMMONS
MARTIN COOK	FRANKLIN KUZENSKI	KEVIN MICHAEL STEPHENS
ALISTAIR DILWORTH	MEENAZ LODHI	MICHAEL J. SULLIVAN
JAN DRAKE	DAVID MACFARLANE	PAUL SUMMERHAYES
BRET DULEY	JAMIE MCFARLANE	JOHN TREADWELL
RAY DUNN	HENRY MARIN	CHRISTOPHER J. VALIN
ROB EDWARDS	CRAIG MARTELLE	PHILIP VAN ITALLIE
RICHARD EYRES	THOMAS MARTIN	JAAP VAN POELGEEST
MARK FERNANDEZ	ALAN D. MCDONALD	FRANCK VAQUIER
CHARLES T FINCHER	JAMES MCGLINCHEY	VORTEX
SYLVIA FOIL	MICHAEL MCMURRAY	DAVID WALTERS JR
GAZELLE OF CAERBANNOG	CHRISTIAN MEYER	MIKE A. WEBER
DAVID GEARY	SEBASTIAN MÜLLER	PAMELA WICKERT
MICHEAL GREEN	MARK NEWMAN	JON WOODALL
BRIAN GRIFFIN	JULIAN NORTH	BRUCE YOUNG

CPSIA information can be obtained
at www.ICGtesting.com
Printed in the USA
BVHW031059290620
582558BV00002B/185